chasing
HOPE

For Taylor –
Best
Wishes!!
Julie C. Lyon

chasing
HOPE

MAYBE THE DEVIL MADE HER DO IT OR WAS IT AN ANGEL?

JULIE C. LYONS

Chasing Hope

Maybe the devil made her do it … or was it an angel?

ISBN: 978-0615808932

Published by:
www.booksforteensbyJulie.com

Table of Contents

Prologue

He pulled into the last parking spot and looked up at the towering office building. Glancing at his watch, he thought, *She's in there, working.*

It would be such an easy thing to do. Get out of the car. Walk into the lobby. Have the man at the front desk page her. *Easy, right?*

The revolving door to the high-rise turned. He froze, hands glued to the wheel. A striking woman in a well-tailored suit emerged from the building. As much as he wanted her to notice him, he also feared her reaction. She proceeded to half-walk, half-jog up Market Street.

As she disappeared into the corner coffee shop, he sat up straight, feeling more disappointed than he wanted to admit, even to himself. *C'mon, it's been months since you did this. Why are you starting up again? Why now?*

But he knew the answer. And with equal certainty, he knew that he would not approach her today. *Not yet.*

He put the folder back into his briefcase and drove away, content with the knowledge that the haunting memories would soon be dead. *Soon… our lives will change forever. And when that happens, neither one of us will ever be the same again.*

CHAPTER 1

Stalking is For Criminals

LILLIAN

What am I doing? She adjusted the sunglasses and pulled the white canvas cap down further to shadow her face.

Only looking.

An imaginary devil and angel were perched precariously on her shoulders, just like in the cartoons.

"Lillian, Lillian, Lillian. You really must stop all this nonsense," Imaginary Angel chided.

"What do you mean?" Imaginary Devil asked as he craned his head and peered at the angel.

"You know – driving through the suburbs to stalk a fourteen-year-old girl!"

Lillian's stomach churned, but Imaginary Devil scoffed, *"Stalking? She's merely looking after her."*

Lillian ended this mental argument the way she always did – by telling herself that Hope was a family member. *Everyone checks in on their loved ones, right?*

She unsuccessfully attempted to push the nagging thoughts to the back of her mind, which caused her to swerve, which caused her to narrowly miss hitting two boys passing a football back and forth in the street. A bead of sweat trickled down her forehead and came to rest above her upper lip. She tried to deny her nervousness, but her trembling hands revealed what she instinctively knew: her life was spinning out of control.

HOPE

"Mom? I'm going over to Karen's house!"

"That's fine," Mom shouted back. "Just call me when you get there!"

I rolled my eyes at her predictable request. *Really, Mom? It's two blocks away. It will take me longer to make the call than to walk there!*

"Okay, Mom. Don't worry. It might take me a whole five minutes to get to Karen's!" Mom has never taken kindly to sarcasm, so I ran out of the house, letting the side door slam shut before she could respond.

I carefully looked up and down the street for approaching cars as I stepped off the curb. Yes, I was an admitted safety freak. Out of nowhere, my brother appeared, running in front of me to intercept a pass from his best friend, Will. I ducked to avoid getting pegged with the football.

"Watch it, Pat! You almost ran me over!"

Patrick ignored me. Of course, he could care less. I don't think my brother thought anything bad would ever happen to him. He was probably right, too, because I've never met a luckier person than Pat. If there's ever a contest, drawing, or game with prizes, Pat would be one of the winners. Mom claimed that she's going to smuggle him into the casinos someday as her talisman. The first time she said that, I asked her what a talisman was, and she told me to look it up.

As the daughter of a teacher, there's one thing I hate about my mother and her friends: they never want to just give you the answer – not even when they know it! Of course, it takes a million times longer to actually search for the information you need, but none of that seems to matter to a teacher.

After flipping through a dictionary, I finally found out that a talisman was, "An object, typically an inscribed ring or stone, thought to have magic powers and to bring good luck."

Ah, yes. My brother, the good luck charm. If he's so charming, what does that make me? I wondered. *I guess I'm the play-it-safe girl. The one who watches out for everything, from crossing the street, to schoolwork, to friendship. And speaking of friends, what did Karen ever see in my brother, anyway?*

Images of Karen Pandora filled my head as I strolled down Vista View Drive. In many ways, Karen was like Patrick – outgoing, outspoken, and always on the lookout for adventure. She never seemed to have any problem meeting new people or making friends. I, on the other hand, spent practically every waking moment so worried about what everyone else thought about me that I never felt entirely comfortable with most of the girls at school, even the ones who were my friends.

But that was about to change.

After discovering a dog-eared copy of a self-help book in the bargain bin at the library's used book sale, something told me this book would be valuable. It was called *Finding Your Voice,* and as I started to read it, my excitement grew. *This is it! The answer I'm looking for...* the answer to finding my way out of my shyness and into a comfort zone with my classmates. Maybe even the answer to becoming more popular, too, though I didn't always admit that goal, even to myself, for fear of being thought of as a shallow person. *There I go again, worrying about everyone else's opinions of me!*

As I approached Karen's block, I tried to recall the advice from Chapter 1. *What was it?* I racked my brain and then remembered it: "Say what you really think – not what others want you to think or say!"

Too busy contemplating the book's advice, I almost didn't notice the car. But when the hair on my neck stood up, I sensed I was not alone. A white sedan trailed dangerously close behind me. Figuring the slow-moving driver wanted to turn onto the street I was crossing, I gave a little wave to indicate that I saw the woman behind the wheel. The car paused briefly at the stop sign and then turned.

As I crossed to the other side, I noticed the car wasn't speeding up. If anything, it was moving more slowly, as if the driver wanted to keep me in her sight. Looking over my shoulder, I could see what looked to be a middle-aged woman gripping the wheel with a large white hat and bug-eyed sunglasses. Even the car was unusual, since most cars in our neighborhood were newer mini-vans and SUV's. This one looked like it came from Rent-a-Wreck, with a smashed-in headlight and huge dent in the roof. I turned around one last time to look at the car that dwarfed the small woman inside of it. The unusual sight fascinated me, from the gray smoke trailing out of the back, to the dents, to the woman's slow driving.

I thought, *Wow, I could do an award-winning imitation of this!*

Not to brag, but I was kind of famous for my imitations, especially the ones of the bitchiest teachers at school. And if there was one thing I noticed since entering high school, it was that there were more miserable teachers to imitate. It wasn't like they had a reason to hate me, either. I wasn't a bad student. In fact, I had been known as a brainiac all through middle school. Unfortunately, being known as the teacher's pet isn't exactly the best way to attract boys or impress friends.

I repeated *Find Your Voice*'s mantra as I walked up to Karen's door and knocked. "Say what you think … say what you think …" I whispered.

Images of the stalker-car faded, and again I wondered why Karen wanted to see me so badly. When my best friend opened the door, she snatched me by the wrist and yanked me into the house, slamming the door behind her.

This news must be major!

LILLIAN

The sight of the blonde hair jolted her back to reality. Not wanting to hit Hope, she pumped her brakes as she approached the stop sign. When the girl turned to look at the car, her stare bore into the dirty windshield, and Lillian slunk down as far as possible in the driver's seat. *Calm down! You're wearing sunglasses and a hat, and you hardly ever drive this car. No one knows you.* The final words cut into her, but she ignored the feelings yet again.

As Hope walked away, Lillian thought about the quizzical look on the girl's face and began to worry. *I've gotta get out of here. If she tells anyone about my car, my license plate – anything! – I won't be able to finish this.*

Though Lillian didn't know what, exactly, she was attempting to finish, she had faith that this was the girl. She was the one.

Hope was the person Lillian was meant to save.

HOPE

"So, what's the big news? You know, we're missing the final episode of *Lost Loves*. Now we'll never get to see if Keith really hated Marilyn all along, or if it was the amnesia that made him turn on her!"

Karen just ignored me and motioned for me to sit at the dining room table. She looked me in the eye before speaking. "I just wanted to tell you that I have an idea. But if I tell you, you have to promise you'll keep it a secret. No matter what. Even if you don't like my plan, you can't tell anyone what I told you, or I'll have to kill you." She laughed, referring to the spy movie we watched yesterday.

"Very funny. So, what's the idea?" I stared back to let her know I was paying attention. "Do you promise? You won't tell anyone?" Karen asked doubtfully.

I pretended to look offended, but I knew why she was so reluctant to share her secret. Last year, I promised Karen I wouldn't tell anyone about her feelings for my brother, but then Karen got really angry with me the next day. Just because I refused to forge her mom's signature on the final exam she failed, Karen started giving me the silent treatment! I tried to explain to her for the millionth time how I wasn't the risk-taker in our friendship, but she didn't care.

So, after two days of steely glares, I stormed into Patrick's room to get revenge. I told him he had a secret admirer.

Though I didn't exactly say Karen's name, Pat eventually asked, "Is it Karen?" I wouldn't answer but instead bobbed my head up and down. Pat groaned, and within two hours, word had gotten back to Karen. It took her almost a month to forgive me. From that day on, I swore to myself that I would never break a friend's trust again. No matter what.

"C'mon, you're my best friend. Spill!"

"Promise first. I know how you are with secrets. And this one's big. Like, we could get arrested if you tell."

Arrested? This must be one helluva secret. A little parental voice in my head scolded me for cursing – even silently! – but I promptly dismissed it to consider Karen's words.

"I have an idea," Karen had said. Maybe she somehow figured out about my self-improvement quest. *Is this a plan to help me break free from my role as Miss Responsible? Her idea could be a first step for me… one small step for Hope, one giant leap for popularity!*

LILLIAN

Hope strolled to the entrance of a large, colonial-style house. Based on her research, this was Karen Pandora's home. Karen, another Roosevelt student, had been a potential target until Lillian decided Hope needed it more. Plus, Hope struck Lillian as open-minded, someone who may be willing to change.

Stop calling them targets, she scolded herself. *Thinking like that, you sound totally crazy.*

Lillian tried to recall the last time her life felt normal, but it was impossible. Years of disorder left her with a flood of memories, all of them unsettling. She thought back to October, the worst month of all. She even had a name for it: The Turning Point.

It had been her third weekend without Paul. With her family living hours away and no close friends to speak of, she felt isolated from the rest of the world. Without the distraction of work, Lillian found herself with too many empty hours to fill. Going on a trip, doing anything that cost money to take her mind off her problems was impossible. She had too much pride to ask Paul for money, and her measly paycheck wouldn't even cover a bus ride.

Daytime television quickly grew tiresome. Lillian needed new companionship. So, that fateful Sunday afternoon, she grabbed the small clock radio and spun the dial, stopping on WFAM 89.2. The Family Station. For an hour, she listened to an inspirational broadcast about a quadriplegic who became a professional musician, thanks to specially-designed instruments. *How can I complain about my failed marriage when this young man has overcome so much more?*

The next program, "R&R with Radio Rev," mesmerized Lillian with the preacher's smooth, southern drawl and hypnotizing voice. The more his words rose and fell like ocean waves, the more she was drawn in. Yes, Lillian liked this radio-church man. This Radio Rev.

Growing up, her parents always said, "Church is for them's that need it." Apparently, Lillian's parents didn't need church, so while the other boys and girls went to Sunday School or Hebrew School, Lillian stayed home. Not being religious seemed alright with Lillian. That is, until she tuned into that spellbinding speaker who called himself Radio Rev.

Now, for the first time in her forty-six years, she felt an interest in religion, in God. Thus began a new weekend pattern for Lillian: wake up, drink a cup of coffee, and quilt. Watch a few hours of television and switch over to the radio at four o'clock. On weekdays, she would race home to catch the broadcast in the comfort of her cozy bungalow, often breaking the speed limit and, once, running a red light to make it to that little silver dial in time. As she opened the leather-bound Bible and sank into her favorite chair, she would think, *This is my new, improved life since the Turning Point.*

With Christmas quickly approaching, Lillian was still listening. And still learning. That learning is what led her to Hope. And that learning is what compelled her to follow Hope every day after school. She took a final glimpse at the Pandora house. Apparently, the girls were staying inside. *Staying safe.*

Soon, she thought, *I'll be given a sign. And then, my plan can begin.*

CHAPTER 2

I Think We Should...

HOPE

"Okay, okay. I promise not to tell. What is it?" I leaned forward on the tall, wooden dining room chair. The antique legs made a loud creaking noise when I sat forward.

Karen ran to the doorway and looked down the hall. "Hello?" she yelled into the air. When no one answered, she sighed. "I guess the coast is clear."

"Karen, just get on with it!" My best friend loved drama, but this was too much!

She spoke so quickly that I could barely understand her. "I think we should sneak over to Miss Lillian's house tomorrow night."

What? "Karen, say it again. Sloooowly."

"IthinkweshouldsneakovertoMissLillian'shousetomorrownight."

Sneak over? Miss Lillian's house?

An image of Miss Lillian, one of our school secretaries, appeared in my mind: the smiling face, the bright clothing. *Definitely the nicest secretary at school.*

And then, there was the whistling. It was so loud it floated into the hall in a haunting way. The first time I heard it, I didn't know what it was, so I had followed the sound into the office.

Trying to be silent, I slid inside and stood as close to the door as possible. She spun around in her office chair, face puckered up and fingers snapping. It sounded like *I've Been Workin' on the Railroad*. Embarrassed, I backed toward the door, but it was too late – Miss Lillian had seen me. She whistled two more notes and stopped to take a breath.

"Hey, Sweetie! How ya doin'? You're Hope, right? From Ms. Tievel's homeroom?" I nodded and felt my face flush. She continued, "So, ya came to hear the concert, did ya?" The way she rushed her words together made it sound like she said "did-cha".

What do I say? My face turned a deeper shade of red, but it didn't matter, because Miss Lillian kept jabbering. "Don't worry, you're not the first person to peek in here to find out where the music's comin' from. I'm like Snow White, you know? Whistle while you work?" She smiled, and I could see her slightly yellowed teeth from too much coffee, too many cigarettes, or both.

"I, umm, just never heard someone who really whistles and works at the same time. That's all," I offered lamely. *For a girl who gets straight A's, that's the best you could do?*

Miss Lillian picked up a monstrous coffee cup with two hands and took a sip. *The coffee must be the dental culprit.*

She smiled, "Well, you've come to the right place. Now, don't be a stranger. I hear you're a mighty fine student, and I don't mind if you stop in for a little listen every now and then. It gets lonely up here. No one but grouchy parents, grouchy secretaries, and a grouchy principal."

I smiled, thinking that Miss Lillian was much friendlier than the secretaries from middle school. At least, that had been my opinion of her until Halloween, when everything about her seemed to change.

⋙◆⋘

Karen interrupted my racing memories with her rapid-fire speaking. "I know, I know. Sneaking out is kind of an immature thing to do, especially to Miss Lillian's house! She's been drier than dirt lately, hasn't she?"

I nodded. Something major must've happened to her because almost overnight, the smile that normally stretched over her face had turned into a tight-lipped grimace. Even her clothes became dull. Brown and gray replaced the bright colors, and the musical office became eerily silent.

"She's boring, alright. Worse than Evil Tievel! But why do you want to sneak into her house?" None of this made sense.

"I've gotta find out if what Anthony told me is true!"

That explains it. Anthony, the new love of her life, could say anything, and she would think it were fascinating. Lately, I noticed that every conversation with Karen could suddenly morph into a discussion about him. And as much as I loved dissecting every conversation, glance, and statement Anthony made, I had my limits. It annoyed me that Karen seemed to forget that I might have a love life - or at least some serious interest in Eli!

But I knew Karen too well. There was no way she would pay attention to me until she finished venting. I had to admit, though, that Karen's current obsession was definitely less awkward than the one she had with Patrick. I thought back to all the times Karen described what she imagined it would be like to hook up with my brother. It wasn't quite as uncomfortable as having your mother try to give you advice about boys and s-e-x (yes, my mom couldn't say the word and literally spelled it out for me!), but I don't necessarily enjoy hearing about my brother's "amazing abs" and otherwise hot body. It's a little too *Flowers in the Attic* for me. *Does Karen think I would ever look at my brother like that?* So, I've been trying to be patient with Karen's focus on her new flavor of the week, grateful that this one wasn't related to me. It was becoming difficult, though. I exhaled, "So, what did Anthony say?"

"That Miss Lillian has a church in her basement!"

"A what?"

Karen confirmed what I thought she said. "A church, Hope! A church!"

CHAPTER 3

The Turning Point

LILLIAN

She took one final glance at Karen's house before checking her phone for messages. No calls. No texts. No voice mails.

What did you expect, Lil? That other people care?

She did the mental calculations again as she looked at the cell phone screen. April 30. *Exactly six months since The Turning Point. Of course, I didn't know it was The Turning Point at the time…*

All she knew at the time was that she couldn't take it anymore. Another broken promise, another broken heart. Though she tried to convince herself that twenty-five years with Paul meant her marriage was working, deep down she knew she was kidding herself. She couldn't even recall what he had done this time to enrage her. All she knew was that this was the last straw.

The blinding anger had scared her almost as much as it had startled Paul. "Leave!" she had screamed. Her voice sounded sure, but inside she trembled. The suitcase handle she gripped became wet from the sweat of her palm.

"Leave? Until when?" Paul had asked that night.

She couldn't answer him because she didn't know the answer. Only Paul knew when he would get help. But right now Paul couldn't think rationally. Lately, anything he said was about as reliable as his beat-up car.

Instead of answering his question, she had pushed the suitcase toward him. Angrily, he had grabbed it and stormed out the door. Though she couldn't be sure, she thought he had mumbled three words under his breath: "I'll be back."

CHAPTER 4

Friends Don't Let Friends Get Arrested

HOPE

"Lemme get this straight. You want to sneak out of my house and spy on –"

Karen cut me off. "Shhh! Do you want the whole neighborhood to hear you? See, this is exactly what I'm talking about. If you aren't telling your brother I like him, you're announcing my plans to the entire neighborhood. I know you're my best friend and all, but you're really pushing it today."

Now that sounded like Mrs. Pandora. She was always telling Karen and her sisters that they were pushing it. It was the code for, "Watch out, because I'm going to freak out, and if that happens, you'll all be grounded!"

Karen and her sisters were always in a state of grounding – they were either earning their way out of being grounded with good behavior, being threatened that they were about to get grounded, or else they were actually grounded. The last scenario only happened if Mrs. Pandora was really angry or if Mr. Pandora (definitely the strict parent) stepped in and put his foot down.

Karen crossed her arms and made a fake coughing sound to grab my attention. "So? Whaddaya think about my idea?"

Normally, I don't like offending people, especially friends. But Chapter 1 of *Finding Your Voice* seemed to be mocking me: *say what you think... say what you think... say what you think...*

I said the first thing that popped into my head. "Karen, that's batshit crazy!"

Karen's mouth dropped open. "Hope, of all people – "

I cut her off. "Y'know, Karen, I'm not as innocent as you think. You're not the only one with a wild side! And you should know that by now...you're my best friend!"

"Wild side? You? Hope, I know that you've been a little – I don't know – different lately. But I mean it in the best way possible! Like, you seem a little more...a little more *real*. Does that make sense?"

I nodded, glad she was noticing my transformation.

She continued, "But you gotta understand, I'm not used to you actually talking like, like...like me! It's a little creepy. I have to admit, though, I kinda like it, too! If you're not Miss Perfect, 24/7, then I don't sound like such a –" She raised her voice to sound like Mrs. Pandora, "You have such a trash mouth, Karen Lynn!" She snickered. "But back to Miss Lillian. What's so crazy about my idea?"

"Spy on someone? Miss Lillian? The secretary? I know she's bizarre, but why would we want to do that? And what do you mean by a church in her house?"

"I don't know for sure, but Anthony said that he was walking by the office and decided to stop in to see if he could get Miss Lillian to start whistling again. He said he was going to get her to whistle a rap song. Isn't that too funny?"

I nodded impatiently to let Karen know she'd better get to the good part, and fast. "The church, Kar? You were talking about the church in her basement?"

"Well, y'know how Miss Lillian always keeps her back to you until she spins around in her chair?"

I nodded, making a motion with my hands, as if to say, "Move along, folks!"

"Impatient today, aren't we? Anyway, she had her back turned, and she was on the phone. Anthony overheard her saying that she should win the tickets because she had a church in her basement and that she'd send them pictures and –"

I cut her off. "Did she say what she meant by a church? And what did he mean, tickets?" All of it sounded too weird. Surely Karen misunderstood.

"I asked Anthony the same questions, and he said Miss Lillian definitely mentioned a church. Plus, she said something like, 'I don't have many people to fill the pews, but I'm working on it!' What else has pews besides a church? Hmmm?"

She had me on that one, but a basement church sounded like a ridiculous concept. "Maybe it's some weird decorating idea. You know, instead of a sports bar or rec room?"

Now Karen grew impatient with me. "Who cares why she did it? I got to thinking, and you know how I get when I've been thinking about something! If this lady's building a church in her basement, I bet she's doing other shady stuff in that house."

"Yeah, like serving Communion or something? C'mon, Karen, I'll admit it's strange, but I don't think it's worth the trouble to break into someone's house. Think about it. You want to risk getting caught by her, the police, or worse yet, your mom? All because Miss Lillian is a little psycho? Plus, church is boring, anyway."

"But, Hope –"

I shook my head to cut her off. Karen looked disappointed, but I knew from the times I had gone to church with my grandparents, the words "excitement" and "church" didn't exactly go hand-in-hand.

LILLIAN

Church. Exciting. A whole new world. At least, it felt that way the more she listened to the "R & R Show". Everything she heard filled her with wonder, but what she loved most about Rev's show was that he never just read the Bible verses. No, he would sloooowly drag his voice over certain words and enunciate others. Then, he would explain what the verse meant in "everyman's words." He liked that phrase a lot, but some nasty critics would call in during his Q&A time and accuse him of being a chauvinist by using the term every*man*.

Radio Rev would just laugh his contagious laugh and explain away his political incorrectness with phrases like, "Our world worries too much about words and not enough about souls," or, "People who like to judge need to learn that the Lord doesn't judge. Why should we?"

Lillian admired the fact that those people couldn't get under his skin. She wasn't like Radio Rev at all. People at work, relatives, and of course, Paul – all of them could cause her stress and anxiety if she feared she let them down.

Listening to Radio Rev convinced her to put an end to her concern about what others thought of her. Instead, following Rev's sermons and keeping her distance from Paul became her new focus.

Whenever Lillian started to doubt her plan, she would call to mind Rev's words, because from what she was learning, anything from the Bible was sure to lead her in the right direction.

What I'm doing is right… right?

HOPE

Try again. I rapped on Karen's head a few times. "Knock, knock! Are you listening to yourself? Think long and hard about this. Your idea could get us A-R-R-E-S-T-E-D. As in, lock us up and throw away the key. Or, at the very least, we could end up in juvenile hall!"

Karen looked at the ceiling – a sure sign she was listening for once. "Well, I can deal with the police, but I definitely don't want to get grounded – again!"

She giggled and fixed her eyes on mine. There was a dreaminess there that worried me. "Think about it, though – this could be the news story of a lifetime – my lucky break!"

Not the "lucky break" again! Karen was always talking about her lucky break. Obsessed with news anchors, it was Karen's dream to become one someday, and she was determined to do whatever it took to make someday arrive sooner.

In her mind, Channel Six would see her talent and decide to break all child labor laws to hire her for the five o'clock news. "That Missy Chang is an airhead anyway," Karen would mumble, referring to the only anchor she disliked.

"What do you have against Missy?" I asked Karen once.

Karen scrunched up her nose. "How can you not hate that lady? I know – she's soooo pretty. But she spends more time flirting with Kurt Johnson than reporting any real news! Plus, when I googled her, I found out she didn't even go to a real school for journalism. Basically, she's an airhead with a good voice and lots of hairspray, but no brains. She probably has to practice reading from the teleprompter, like, a million times!"

Karen was infatuated with Kurt Johnson, the baby-faced reporter who worked opposite Missy. Kurt and Missy would joke around with each other, and Missy would always laugh hysterically at Kurt's jokes (side note: the jokes aren't even funny).

Missy obviously liked Kurt; even my mom noticed it one evening. She muttered, "Ugh, such blatant innuendo! I thought Channel Six had higher standards!"

I knew better than to ask my mom what "blatant" and "innuendo" meant, so off to the dictionary I went. Blatant: "very obvious." Innuendo: "a double meaning by playing on a possibly sexual interpretation of an otherwise innocent uttering." Made sense – Missy was so obviously flirting with Kurt that even my mom noticed!

But back to Karen and her plan. This sounded like another one of her impulsive schemes that was sure to get both of us in trouble.

"Karen, don't you remember the last time you had a scoop?"

"You mean the woods fire?" she asked innocently.

I glared at her. "What else would I be talking about?" Who could forget that one?

It had been a cloudy September day three years ago when five fire trucks screamed by my house, on their way to what we later found out was a fire in the woods. As the flashing lights passed my house, Karen raced toward the front door. In a hysterical voice, she screamed, "Let's go! Let's go! Bikes! No time for helmets! Where's my camera?"

Off we went, following the trucks, skidding to a halt, hiding in the bushes. Something told me we were about to get in trouble. I had shared my concerns with Karen, who just shook her head and patted me on the back.

"All good reporters do this sometimes," Karen whispered. That was the first and last time she would convince me of what "real reporters" do. Even if it were true, she forgot to tell me that if there are any real reporters who do this, they probably get yelled at by the picky lady whose yard we were in.

No sooner had we kneeled behind a lush line of shrubs than we heard a high-pitched voice. It sounded like someone drew a steak knife across a porcelain plate very slowly. It didn't take a genius to realize the lady was screeching at us: "You two! Don't pretend you don't see me, Miss Camera and Little Miss Pink Shirt!"

I looked down. *Pink shirt? Check. Karen holding her camera? Check. Guess she means us, so we'd better….*

"I asked, what are you two doing, trespassing on my property? I just had this lawn thatched and seeded, and I don't need you two hooligans ruining it."

We weren't laughing, but she continued, "Oh, so you think this is funny? Well, look who's going to be laughing when your parents get the bill from my landscaper! I'm sure two hundred dollars is no laughing matter! But then again, I'm sure your parents will just write a check. Kids these days never get punished. No, they just keep making mistakes and waiting for their parents to pick up the broken pieces. And another thing about kids these days…."

Obviously, this was the much-talked-about neighborhood witch, Ms. Parker. All Hidden Hills kids with any brains knew better than to trespass on her property, and Karen and I clearly weren't thinking that day. Though I had seen Ms. Parker many times directing landscapers and handymen to keep her house as well-maintained as a private country club, I never heard her speak. We had never been the object of her hatred before, either.

As we skittered away from her house, I turned to look. Ms. Parker had a faraway look in her eyes, kind of like when Karen's preparing to share yet another Anthony story, so I had grabbed her by the shirt and pulled her down the sidewalk. I figured if we stayed for round two of "kids these days," our parents would definitely receive a phone call.

"Aww, now we won't get the close-up footage! See? They have the whole area blocked off." I looked up and saw what Karen was referring to: the firemen had put up yellow Caution tape so that no one could get close to the fire.

"Let's just go, Kar. No story is worth this much trouble." Reluctantly, Karen let me lead her away from what she was sure was the scoop that would gain her fame and fortune.

Now, here she was again, talking about her big break. She scoffed, "Oh, Hope, don't be such a worrier! I promise, no Ms. Parker this time! Miss Lillian's harmless. How dangerous can it be?"

I resented Karen's accusation. *Don't be such a worrier.* As much as I envied Karen's adventurousness, and as much as I knew taking risks was the only way to overcome my fears, the cautious side of me was winning out. Something told me if I listened to Karen, things would not end well.

It was time to convince her that this was a very bad idea.

"Karen? Look at me. Good. Think about what you're saying. Miss Lillian is definitely weird, and she's been super-strange for the past month. I guess our first impressions of her were wrong, or she changed, or both."

"But –"

I continued, "Karen, the reason she's changed doesn't really matter! What matters is that her basement is none of our business."

Karen opened her mouth to speak, but I refused to give her the courtesy of a reply. "Listen, it doesn't sound like Anthony had a lot of information. I know you like him, but you've got to admit he exaggerates! Even if what he said is true, what could you do about it? She didn't give you permission to be at her house, so Channel Six won't be able to cover the story anyway."

When Karen remained silent, I added, "You know how this would end: if we got caught, my mom and dad would have to drive you home, and you would get grounded…again!"

Karen looked at me for several moments before speaking. *Another good sign.*

"Hmmm, I hate to say it, Hope, but you're probably right." She sighed. "I just wish I knew what she was talking about. Like, does she have Sunday services in there? Is there some big, ancient pipe organ? Does she have tons of Bibles? I keep picturing all these wooden pews with velvety cushions and a stray dog sitting in the middle of them."

I looked at her with questions in my eyes. "Stray dog?"

Karen sighed impatiently. "Think about it. She seems lonely and eccentric. Doesn't the dog make sense? To keep her company?" I nodded and she continued. "And there would be some old, gray pastor standing up front saying stuff like, 'Please don't mind the dog. He lives upstairs, and he just so happens to enjoy praying. Amen.'"

We both giggled as we envisioned Miss Lillian, a pastor, and a wayward dog going to basement church. Definitely a funny picture!

CHAPTER 5

WFAM

LILLIAN

The pastor's voice boomed through the radio speakers and filled the interior of the white sedan. She began to relax, and her small hands stopped clutching the wheel. The houses on Vista View Drive became a blur as she drove down the tree-lined boulevard. The dashboard clock flashed 4:07. Commercials were over, and the sermon was starting.

Almost immediately, she felt the trance begin. She didn't fully understand what happened when he spoke, but something in the evangelist's voice always put her into a dreamlike state.

Today, the reverend discussed living life like a real Christian:

"Surely, there's lots of folks out there who call themselves Christians, but they're just playing 'dress-up,' as I like to say." The pastor chuckled, and Lillian smiled at his down-home speech. Radio Rev was the type of man who could speak to people and make them feel like he had traveled through the airwaves to sit next to the listener as he meandered through his lengthy sermons. Those charming mannerisms drew in a heavy listening crowd on WFAM every day at four o'clock, and Lillian could understand why. The corners of her mouth curled into a knowing grin as she thought about all the people she knew who were playing Christian dress-up.

Radio Rev continued, "Don't get me wrong. I do believe these well-meaning believers really think they are good Christians. They think about their good deeds and how they go to church every Sunday. They even put some bucks in the ol' offering plate! Sounds pretty good, doesn't it?"

He paused, as if he were allowing the listener to nod in agreement during the silent space. "But remember what Jesus said in the Book of Romans: 'But to the one who does not work, but believes in Him who justifies the ungodly, his faith is reckoned as righteousness.' Folks, this is just a fancy way of sayin'…."

She had noticed that he loved to cut off the g's in his speech before he made an important point, "It is your faith that gets ya inta Heaven, and without that, no amount of good works matter a lick if ya ain't got faith in ol' J.C.!"

It was now 4:25, which was the time that Radio Rev really drove the point home. Lillian turned the knob on the radio to the right to let the entire car fill with the deep voice:

"But remember, folks, that's not all! No, by golly, it's not. Of course, faith is all you need for Heaven, but why be selfish and keep others out of the loop? Why not let them in on the secret? Why not save some souls along the way? The apostle Paul made it clear that, as true Christians, we are called to follow the Great Commission. Remember that one? Sure ya do! I know, the Bible can get all fancy on us plain folk, but Paul commissioned us – or committed us – to share the Good News with everyone. Everyone. Let me say that one more time… everyone. Is this an easy task? Of course not! Will everyone hear our testimonies and say, 'Why, thank you, Sir. Thank you, ma'am, you just saved my eternal soul?' If you excuse my French…heck, no! Lots of nonbelievers out there will ridicule you and tell you that you're dead wrong. But remember this: *you* know the truth. You know the *secret*. And if they don't want to listen, I weep for 'em. I pray for 'em. And I won't give up on a single one of 'em. I'll keep tryin', and 'keep on keepin' on.' Heh, heh."

Rev chuckled ever-so-softly. "Beloved listeners, know this. You are doing the right thing. So, all you Christians – you real Christians – keep on keepin' on, and save a soul today. Amen."

Lillian murmured "Amen" at the same time and mentally calculated how much money she could donate this month. Radio Rev was explaining how to make online donations, but she tuned out, already knowing how to send the money. *Maybe I can cut back on the groceries a bit this month? If I do, I could probably send an extra twenty or thirty dollars.*

She pulled into her driveway, thinking of Hope. Even though she kept telling herself it was the angel part of her that came up with the plan, the image of a devil plagued her thoughts.

My idea is good. Really good, she thought as she opened her front door and climbed over the pile of envelopes the mailman had dropped through the door slot. The Reverend's words echoed in her head along with her plan, like the reverberation of a cymbal after the crash.

He said we need to save everybody. Everyone. No matter the price. Keep on keepin' on…

RADIO REV

"Amen." Radio Rev closed his eyes.

"That's a wrap, RR! I don't ever remember so many callers, do you?" Suzanne asked.

Radio Rev looked at the station manager and tried to grin, but grinning was not an innate skill of his. *Too many years of being a serious preacher's son will do that to you,* Rev thought to himself.

He broke the silence. "If I get one more request for free tickets to this weekend's revival, I am going to screeeeam."

Suzanne laughed. "Look at it this way, RR, you're a popular guy. Even though they won't get to see you, they're willing to pay to hear you! In fact, Lil' Lady called again today."

"Hmm?" Rev was only half-listening. Suzanne was known to babble incessantly, and he had learned long ago that the best way to handle the prattle was to make polite noises and wait for the storm of words to pass.

Suzanne droned on until he heard the phrase "church-in-the-basement." Rev looked up. "I'm sorry, Suzanne, I missed that last part. Still thinking about the sermon, I guess. What did you say?"

Suzanne exhaled slowly and repeated herself. "I said, Lil' Lady called again. Remember her? The one with the church in her basement? The same one who's called almost every day for the past two weeks? Well, today she was absolutely begging to get into the drawing for the revival tickets."

"And? Your point?" *Time to wrap up the story.*

Suzanne looked flustered but continued, "Well, you would've thought she lost her best friend when I told her the contest was over. But then I told her about the free sunrise service, and I had to hold the phone away from my ear. That woman's got a set of lungs on her!"

She paused and took a sip of her coffee. "I think I burst her bubble, though, when I explained that preaching in person meant it would be with your voice only. I don't know, Rev, maybe you should consider showing that face of yours… I'll bet people would pay extra money if they knew they'd get to hear the voice and see you!"

Rev looked startled for a split second, but just as quickly regained composure. "I know, I know. Everyone loves to tell me how I should put myself out there, whatever *that* means. It's just another example of our instant gratification society. If people can't have it their way, right away, they're bellyaching and moaning about how no one is meeting their needs. Boo, hoo!"

At this point, the conversation was effectively over. He knew it, and Suzanne knew it. Rev seldom responded to Suzanne's musings with more than a sentence or two. She would understand that his mini-scolding signified the end of their discussion. He also knew from experience that after his lecture, she would be super-sweet for the next few days and not ask too many questions.

The Rev didn't particularly like lecturing a thirty-five year old mother of two. Heck, she was basically his age! But he knew that setting people straight was necessary at times. It was especially vital when people poked around and tried to figure out his real name, his real job, or anything related to his past. In those instances, Rev averted the nosy questions with his biting words and sharp tongue. It always worked, and the Rev knew it had to work, for two important reasons. First, if anyone knew who he really was, it would ruin his ability to stay in his day job. Second, if people pried into his past, then it would force him to think about his family—and Caroline.

Thinking about Caroline was not an option. It would never be an option.

If there's too much gray in my life, I can't be the black and white pastor I need to be – that my listeners need me to be. And, then, I would lose all my power.

HOPE

Karen sighed and said, "You and your common sense, Hope! I guess I'll put my journalism career on hold...again. But couldn't we just –"

I interrupted: "I've got two words for you: Ms. Parker. Isn't that reason enough to stop thinking about Miss Lillian?"

"Okay, okay! You win." She began pacing back and forth. "Well, if we don't have that to look forward to, what are we going to do at your house tomorrow night?"

Just as I was about to speak, something moved outside Karen's window. I looked closer. All I saw was a car at the curb. Then I did a double-take because it wasn't just any old car – it was the tired-looking station wagon from before!

"Ooh, Karen, look out your window – quick!"

Karen sprinted toward the window.

"Duck, so she doesn't see you!"

Karen crouched down as instructed. "So who doesn't see me?"

"The driver! Follow me." I ran over to the window and kneeled. All anyone would see from the outside was the top of my head and my eyes.

Karen followed suit. She said in a stage whisper, "Who is it?"

I whispered back, "Why are we whispering? She's outside!" We both laughed as we watched the car pull away from the curb and move slowly down the street.

In a normal voice I continued, "I almost forgot to tell you about this lady and her car…."

With that, I launched into my imitation of the mysterious driver. I grabbed a decorative plate from the end table and pretended it was the steering wheel.

In a shaky voice, I whined, "Oh, my dearie! What do we have here? A girl walking to her friend's house? Let's see if I can get close enough to hit her! Hee, hee, hee!"

Karen gaped. "Did she hit you?"

"No, but she was getting close!"

Then I spotted the finishing touch: Karen's sunglasses that practically covered my entire face. "And she had on these enormous sunglasses," I began, "and a hat – do you have a white hat?" Karen stopped laughing long enough to shake her head no, so I continued driving my imaginary car, bumping into the sofa as if it were a parked car, and then saying, "Sorry, girls, I gotta go. Time to return my ride to rent-a-wreck! Woo-hoo, what a joy ride that was!" I made my voice sound weak and wobbly.

Karen laughed, "So, did she really say any of that stuff?"

"Naw, I'm just giving the story 'vivid details', like Ms. Tievel says." In addition to being my homeroom teacher, Ms. Tievel is also our English teacher who never accepts our compositions unless we include "vivid details."

"Yeah, Ms. Parker sure is a vivid – " Karen stopped as my cell phone vibrated, crawling across the dining room table. I glanced at the text: "where r u?"

Uh, oh. I forgot to call Mom!

I do respect the fact that my mom has tried to get on board with the texting thing, but sometimes she can be really annoying. Like right now. I mean, did she truly think something horrible happened to me in the past ten minutes?

I clicked the keys: "sorry 4got 2 call @ kar's b home @ 6?"

"OK but next time pls call i wz frantic!!!"

My mom loves the exclamation point, especially coupled with the word "frantic". Thankfully, she wasn't "frantic!!!" enough to force me to return home for a lecture on how, "In this day and age, with such wonderful technology, there is no reason to keep a parent waiting and wondering where his or her child is!"

She must have had a good day at school, because when her students were bad – watch out! Any small infraction at home would be met with long lectures and stern stares.

Doesn't she get tired of lecturing? I'd sometimes wonder. *Or maybe,* I reasoned, *it's such a habit that she can't help herself when she gets home!*

Karen tapped her foot as I texted. I glared at her. "I'm almost finished. Just give me a minute, already!" She took the hint and walked across the room to an old radio. She flipped it on and mindlessly rolled the tuner through the different stations. On one of her pauses, a man's loud voice echoed through the speakers.

"What is that?"

We listened for a few minutes to the commanding voice. Whoever it was kept saying "Amen" over and over.

"Must be one of those angel lists," Karen murmured.

"Angel what?"

"Angel lists. You know, those religious guys who say a few prayers and expect you to send them your life savings?"

I thought for a minute. Finally, the word came to me. "Don't you mean evangelists?"

A pained expression crossed Karen's face. "Okay, I get it. I'm not as smart as you, Miss Vocabulary. Believe me, my parents never let me forget that fact!"

I did my best to make her feel better. "C'mon, I'm not showing off. The only reason I know about evangelists is because my grandparents like watching them on TV. I guess that's where I heard it."

Apparently bored with my explanation, Karen abruptly switched off the radio and launched into a monologue about what we could do at my house Friday night. Since "breaking and entering" wasn't on her list, I sat back, nodded my head at the right times, and felt thankful for inheriting common sense from my dad. Clearly, logic and reasoning weren't part of the Pandora gene pool.

CHAPTER 6

Save a Soul

LILLIAN

Lillian hid the hat and sunglasses in a drawer. *Why do I feel like I have something to hide? I'm just checking in on a loved one,* Lillian argued with herself.

She tried to refocus on Radio Rev's sermon from a few minutes ago, but it was useless. Her mind kept drifting to the image of Hope Minor, looking over her shoulder with curiosity and fear. She settled down on the bed and kicked off her shoes. With her head on a quilted pillow, she thought, *Hope—afraid of me? How could that be? Hope is my chosen one, that's all. That's all…*

⇒⋆⇐

She thought back to that fateful day. November 21, to be exact. Lillian had been sitting at her desk, sipping her beloved extra-caffeinated Donut World coffee and reading Radio Rev's daily calendar of quotes, *The Best of Radio Rev: 365 Thoughts for Our Walk with God.*

A petite, freckled freshman entered the office timidly. No swagger, no attitude, nothing that would indicate she was here to see Mr. Vambles for some school code infraction.

Lillian recognized the girl as Hope Minor, an honors student whose mother also happened to teach in the district. Hope had popped into the office a few times earlier in the year, but Lillian hadn't seen her around lately. *I guess I haven't exactly been Ms. Social, either.*

Almost daily, Radio Rev demanded that his listeners share his message with others. *SAS – Save a Soul,* he called it. Lillian would sit in the office and, during quiet moments, wrack her brain trying to figure out who really needed saving. All the other secretaries went to church, and even if they weren't following Rev's messages to the letter, Lillian knew from their disgruntled attitudes that they'd be too opinionated to listen to her, a mere colleague. No, the SAS wasn't meant for them. Of that Lillian was convinced.

She looked up at Hope and then back down at her daily calendar of Radio Rev's quotes. Today's was "The soul you save may be your own, but isn't it nice to save others, too?" As she looked up at Hope, something clicked. *Hope* was the answer she'd been looking for! *I didn't have to go out and find the soul to save… it found me!*

"May I help you?" Lillian asked, her voice trembling with anticipation.

"I haven't heard your whistling lately…" Hope's voice trailed off, as if she were embarrassed. Lillian would need to put the girl at ease.

"Oh, well, ummm, things have been kind of hectic lately. But enough about me. How about you? Are things hectic in your life?"

Hope looked a bit startled but answered politely. "Yeah, well, it's always busy in our house because my brother plays, like, a gazillion sports. We're constantly driving to his hockey games, baseball practices, and soccer tournaments. I don't like sports all that much, either, so it's kinda boring."

Lillian tried to focus on Hope's words, but it was difficult. *I finally found a soul to save!*

"Well, y'know, I've found a really good way to pass the time when I'm bored," she began.

Hope raised her eyebrows. "Really? How?"

"I pray."

Hope wrinkled her nose. "Huh?"

Lillian began speaking quickly, trying to cram her message into a neatly-packaged present, a gift for Hope and her everlasting soul. But what came out was: "Yes, Hope, prayer…I just talk to God…don't you talk to God?…I mean in a passing time kind of way?…I mean, it's so serene and really helps my nerves and…well, not that you have a nerve problem, but…you do get straight-A's and that's gotta be stressful, and…" she stopped speaking and simply asked, "You do pray, don't you?"

Hope shifted back and forth from left to right foot. Lillian felt like she were on a boat. "Umm, yeah, I guess. I mean, we pray a lot at my grandmother's church, but we only go there a few times a year, so… umm, I think I need to go. Yeah, that's it. I'm supposed to meet Karen. That's right…catch ya later!" And with that, she dashed out of the office.

Lillian blinked. *Did I come on too strong?*

All morning, she replayed the conversation over and over in her mind. Each time, she berated herself more sternly for not getting it right. Radio Rev never would have made a fool of himself like that.

RADIO REV

Sitting in his study, he mindlessly glanced through the stack of papers the station president had shoved in his hands after the broadcast. He had just walked out of the studio, leaving an open-mouthed Suzanne in his wake. *She probably still can't figure me out…and I can't blame her. Sometimes even I don't know who I am.*

In many ways, Radio Rev knew this was merely a persona: this fire-and-brimstone pastor was not the real him. But when he started the radio show, his parents finally accepted him, and his father's proud proclamations to the congregation about "my son up North" turned him into a hometown hero for following in his father's footsteps. That level of acceptance was something he couldn't readily give up, especially when he thought about Caroline and their time together.

No, the person Caroline tried to bring out in him needed to be dead and buried, and the only way he could stay on the straight and narrow was to keep up with this weekly façade.

Stop calling it a facade, Glenn, he scolded himself. *This is who God wanted you to be.*

He shook his head as he thought, *OK, maybe God doesn't want me to be exactly like this, but my parents do, my friends do, and it feels so good! For once, everyone loves me! Well, almost everyone. Everyone except...*

He glanced at the innocent-looking file folder on his desk. Glenn picked it up and looked at the tab, simply titled "C". When he opened the folder, photos and articles from her column in the *Philadelphia Times* slipped onto the desk.

As he re-read the familiar words, he thought for the millionth time that he really should leave New Jersey and head south. Head for home. But that would seal his fate. Permanently. There was no way she would ever move back there, so if he left his options open, there was the outside chance he could leave this life and pick up where he left off almost twenty years ago.

The thought of the two of them getting back together brought tears to his eyes. He wiped them away with an impatient hand. *Glenn, you're such a wuss! How would that ever happen? You ruined it, and she's moved on. Facts are facts.*

Glenn discovered that distraction was the best way to take away the pain, and in many ways the radio show lessened the heartache. He reasoned, *How could I be heartbroken when I have a hometown that loves me?* But he knew the answer: *They wouldn't love me if they knew the real me, so this is what I give them, and it gets me through my days.*

CHAPTER 7

Most Popular

HOPE

I shuffled through the papers in my backpack and pulled out the neon-colored announcement: "Roosevelt Dance: Friday Night! All proceeds benefit the Student Council's spring trip."

The spring trip to New York City was the main reason so many of us wanted to serve as a homeroom representatives for Student Council in the first place. In addition to proving your popularity, becoming a rep meant that you missed three days of school to go to The Big Apple (our principal's words, not mine). Stories of late nights at an amazing five-star hotel, celebrity sightings, and no parents made the New York trip a highly coveted experience.

Karen and I ran for Student Council in September, but with Maddie Braun and Krystal Gambill as competitors, we didn't stand a chance. When the not-so-surprising election results were announced, Karen and I counted ourselves out of the New York trip for this year, at least.

Maddie Braun hadn't always been student-government-popular. Most of us who had known her since kindergarten found her constant bragging irritating: as one of the richest girls I've ever known, Maddie has never hesitated to show off her designer labels or to tell everyone how much her parents spent on her.

So even though most girls have always hated Maddie, she quickly earned popularity points with the boys three years ago when she announced to the entire cafeteria that she was wearing a bra because she was "developing". I'm sure if someone confronted her at the time, she would have claimed she was only telling her clique, but her loud voice was a dead giveaway that she intended for everyone – and I mean everyone! – to hear her.

"Y'know, Cecilia's Secret is, like, so gauche," she had practically screamed. She seemed to know she was talking above her listeners with her vocabulary, because when one of them asked, "What's gauche mean, Maddie?" she beamed and raised her nose just a little bit higher in the air.

"Oh, it just means, like, unsophisticated. My Mother swears by La Diamant bras, so that's what I'm wearing! They're really expensive, but sooooo comfortable."

Then, she granted the girls a peek by pulling her expensive T-Shirt down so everyone within a ten-foot radius could see the tiniest bit of cleavage and the edge of a lacy-looking bra. That caught the boys' eyes, and by seventh grade, Maddie had earned herself the dual title of richest *and* most popular girl.

Then there's Krystal, the other Student Council rep from our homeroom. She's not rich, but as one of Maddie's followers, Krystal brings a biting sarcasm to the group that keeps everyone on their toes. Not only will she make fun of people's clothes, but she'll make fun of someone's house, intelligence (or lack thereof), and siblings. Ironically, Krystal's home, IQ, and sister are all rather lacking. *Probably makes fun of people before they can beat her to it.*

I walked over to the small makeup mirror on my vanity. In the bright lights, I could see every pore on my face. I knew I wasn't ugly, despite some pimples and other small imperfections. *So who decides who's popular and who's not? And why do I care, anyway?*

Grabbing the copy of *Finding Your Voice,* I turned to the quiz at the beginning of the book: "How Strong is Your Voice?" I reviewed my results, which weren't solid like my school grades. Rather, the quiz revealed that I needed to "improve self-confidence" and "establish a unique identity, regardless of trends and others' opinions."

I thought about Krystal and Maddie again. I wondered if they worried about everyone else's opinions, or if their seemingly effortless cool factor was natural. And even though I knew going to the dance on Friday would benefit them and their fellow student council-mates, I knew Karen and I would attend, just like everyone else in the freshman class.

CHAPTER 8

Painful Memories

LILLIAN

Lillian Amadon looked at herself in the mirror. *Not bad,* she thought, *for someone who only got two hours of sleep last night.*

Another sleepless night. Another night of arguments. Not arguments in person, thankfully, but phone arguments with her soon-to-be ex-husband.

She saw the now-familiar reflection of tears in her red-rimmed eyes. The dark circles that formed craters under her eyes couldn't completely mask her attractive face. The previous night's episode of *How You've Done Me Wrong, Lillian!* repeated itself in her head. *Thanks, Paul,* she thought wryly.

The ringing phone punctuated the air and interrupted her thoughts. The caller ID clearly read Paul.

Paul? Again? She couldn't make up her mind. All of the muscles in her neck and chest contracted as she allowed the phone to ring five, six, seven times. An eerie silence followed. Paul wouldn't give up that easily.

Sure enough, the shrill ring pierced the silence mere seconds later. Lillian half-tiptoed, half-slid across the kitchen floor. Approaching the phone, she touched it with her fingertips. She paused, weighing the pros and cons of answering.

If I answer, it'll be the continuation of last night's monologue (or as Lillian began to think of them, Paul-o-logues). But if I don't answer, he's going to open that first beer or down that first shot. Then another. And another. And he'll call back again later. Say, around 10:00 PM, like last night, and I'll be stranded in the house on the phone with a drunk for hours. Maybe I should just get it over with.

Her fingers encircled the receiver. "Hello?"

"Lillian, that you?" Paul asked. Even though she lived alone and no one else ever picked up the phone in her house, whenever Paul called he would ask her to identify herself.

"Yes, Paul, it's me. What do you want?" Lillian measured her words and tone carefully. Any small misstep could lead to phone call disaster, and she had to make this conversation quick.

"What happened to the keys for the shed? I need some tools for this broken sink. You know, the sink in this miserable apartment you've banished me to. You never gave me the spare key."

His accusation hung in the air, ready for Lillian to respond to if she desired. Over the years, the negativity that had once festered was now explosive, and Lillian knew if Paul wasn't raising his voice, it was a good sign. She wasn't about to tap into his bottomless reserves of anger.

"Paul, I gave you the spare key, remember? When you stopped by last weekend to pick up the TV? I taped it to the top of the set." Lillian held her breath, hoping the keys were still there so that Paul wouldn't have yet another excuse to stop by the house.

"What? On the TV set? Lemme see...." Static and a bump filled her ears. Lillian could picture Paul dropping the phone on the end table of his tiny apartment. She heard what she guessed were footsteps moving towards the TV. From a distance, she could hear his deep voice: "Ohhh, yeah." The voice got louder as he spoke into the phone: "Got it,

Lil. You were right, they were on the TV. One of the few things you've been right about lately, huh?"

Lillian ignored the insult. She knew enough not to take the bait, not to justify herself, no matter how right she believed herself to be. *You can't argue with an addict*, she learned from the support group she attended weekly. The leader's words echoed in her head: *Even though he'll try to bargain with you and make you think you're the crazy one, remember that he's caught in the grip of a monster. You need to protect yourself.*

She also knew that Paul, for all of his faults, was not prone to physical violence, even after he'd been drinking all evening with his buddies at Sports-N-More down the road. His words, however, were another thing altogether. In all their years of marriage, Lillian learned that the more Paul drank, the uglier his face and words became, until his mumblings transformed into a gnarled garble of half-words and sounds.

"Cat got yer tongue, Lil? What's with the silent treatment?"

She couldn't win. If she responded to Paul or tried to explain herself, he would intensify the argument, and if she remained quiet, he would accuse her of being passive-aggressive. Time to end the conversation.

"Paul, I'm glad you found the keys. Really. Listen, I don't mean to be rude, but I'm going to have to go. I have a meeting tonight."

"How come you always have time for your meetings but no time for me, Lil?" He sneered through the phone when he said the word meetings.

The meetings that Paul hatefully referred to were group counseling sessions she started attending in January. They were designed for people involved in unhealthy relationships. The counselor called it co-dependent, but Lillian could care less what it was called. All she knew was that the group was the only hope she had to break free from Paul's domineering ways. The strength from the group fortified Lillian weekly, giving her strength in some of her weakest moments. Like right now.

She felt the familiar stab of guilt for letting Paul down again, but then she remembered what everyone kept telling her – Paul was trying to blame her for his problems, and if she agreed to take the blame, she would prevent him from admitting he had a problem in the first place.

Her heart felt like a hand was squeezing it. "Paul, I can only control myself, not you, as I've already told you. These meetings are helping me to heal, and I wish with all my heart that you would find a place to help yourself, too."

As much as she didn't want to mean it – didn't want to still care, she admitted to herself that her words were sincere. She still loved this man.

She held her breath, unsure of Paul's reaction. It was like playing on a see-saw, waiting to see who would upset the balance. That feeling definitely wasn't helping with the ulcer the doctor found in her stomach a few months ago.

As Paul spoke, she recalled the well-meaning advice from the counselor about "healthy boundaries." *It all makes sense,* Lillian thought, *but why do I feel like small pieces of my heart are ripping apart when I hear the anger and pain in Paul's voice?* In these moments, her resolve to use tough love weakened. Paul sensed it.

His voice softened, which put Lillian on guard. "You're right, Lil. I probably should go talk to someone, but things are so busy at the office right now. I'm sure next month will get better, so you can stop worrying about me!" Wistfully, he added, "In fact, how 'bout I swing by, and we can grab a bite to eat?"

Even though she was feeling very alone at the moment, she knew she couldn't give in. Not yet. "I'm so sorry, but I really can't miss this meeting, Paul. Please try to understand. This is something I have to do – alone. And I do mean it when I say that I pray for you every night. I truly want you to get better."

She meant it. She wouldn't have married Paul if she hadn't fallen in love with the impish smile of his, his way of making her feel like she was the only person in the world. She never would have dropped out of college to start working in the real world to help put Paul through Gettysbury College if he wasn't truly special. That Paul was gracious for her support. Driven. Motivated. That was the Paul she loved. Not the man he turned into after a night of drinking. But she knew that until he got help, Paul would be both men – her own version of Jekyll and Hyde. She hoped that her denial to see him wouldn't bring out Hyde, but she knew any refusal on her part could potentially lead to his flip side.

"Fine," Paul seethed. His voice sounded steely, like a guitar string being tightened as far as it would go. "Go to your... meeting," he snarled. "Just know that if you don't have time for me, I'll probably call Bob."

Bob was Paul's most loyal friend and drinking buddy – when Bob was employed, that is. Bob's seriously-lacking work ethic dated back to their college days, and it caused him to lose most jobs before the second paycheck. However, when Bob had a job and paycheck, he was sure to spend most of it at Sports-N-More with Paul. As for the rest of the money, he spent most of it on his guns. The *Eat, Sleep, HUNT* hat he wore advertised Bob's priorities. The only part Lillian doubted was that sleep came in second place instead of first, because if Bob wasn't sitting on a barstool after work, he could be found passed out in a La-Z-Boy recliner in front of his television set, tuned to the Outdoor Life Network.

Lillian wasn't going to cave in. Paul's threat about going to the sports bar with Bob was an obvious ploy. Paul knew that she worried that one of these days Paul or Bob would wrap his car around a lamp post after hours of telling their tales of woe to Mike, the Sports-N-More bartender.

Paul voiced a few more empty threats, but eventually Lillian was able to end the conversation. She knew it would only be a matter of time before Paul would call back, and Lillian didn't want to be around for that.

She scurried around the small kitchen, making herself a Cup O'Soup before the 7:00 meeting. *For once, I wish I didn't have any problems to discuss! Then I could sit and listen to the other women's dilemmas and pretend that I didn't have those problems, too.*

Deep down, Lillian knew she *did* have those problems, and no amount of wishing was going to change that. *But a prayer might.*

She ran upstairs, knelt by her bedside, and prayed, "Dear Lord, please give me strength to do the right thing with Paul. I love him dearly, but I want the healthy Paul, not the man he is right now. Grant me the wisdom to see through his lies and trust that You will guide me and care for me. Amen."

It was a short prayer, she knew, but heartfelt and honest. She looked at the clock. It was 6:45. *It's time.* Lillian grabbed the keys and walked out to her car.

Hmm, I really need to take care of that dent. She looked at the old white Lincoln and sighed. *I guess my next paycheck will go towards the repair, instead of the revival tickets. I wish Paul would bring the truck back. I hate his car.*

RADIO REV

He looked more closely at the WFAM paperwork. Pages and pages of timetables, floor plans for the speakers, lights, and sound system. Most of it had nothing to do with Radio Rev's sermon at the revival, but the inch-thick pile indicated how seriously the station was taking this event. *Dad never did anything this big,* he thought smugly.

⋙◆⋘

While it was true that Rev was the son of a pastor, that was where the similarities between father and son ended. Where his father was a soft-spoken man, Glenn had determined himself to be loud, commanding and strong in everything he did. As a young boy, he noticed how the parishioners took advantage of his dad's generosity and patience. Sometimes even Glenn felt guilty for exploiting his father's compassion, knowing he wouldn't have to worry about getting yelled at or beat like most of his friends.

As a typical preacher's kid, Glenn spent a good part of his youth rebelling against everything he was brought up to believe and do. But every bad choice he made seemed petty in comparison to his life-changing decision during senior year...

Her name was Caroline, and even twenty years later, Rev could envision her smiling face. "Caroline, for Carolina," he would joke with her. The first time he said that, her eyes opened wide with astonishment. She laughed and said, "People in this town can be dumb as a stump! Do you know that you're the first person in Mountwell to figure out where my mama got my name? She always wanted to live there, y'know. And no one ever connected my name to the state...except for you! That's why you're my darlin' Glennie."

My darlin' Glennie. How he'd loved that pet name, corny as it was. To be honest, he loved everything about Caroline – her laugh, her flashing blue eyes, the freckled nose that got sunburned too easily, her brilliant mind. Plus, she was completely different from the girls he grew up with. Most folks from his town were God-fearing, simple folk who worked hard, got married, had kids, raised a family, and spent their evenings sitting on neighbors' porches talking about home and church. Nobody moved out of Mountwell, Georgia, and nobody moved in. Usually. But when Caroline's family came to town, Glenn's world was forever changed.

The first time he met her, she was sitting in front of him in chemistry class, humming. Not loud enough for the teacher to hear, but loud enough for Glenn to recognize the strains of Led Zeppelin. These certainly weren't the church hymns he was used to hearing. Amidst the humming, she somehow managed to listen intently to the teachers and constantly raise her hand to contribute. And contribute she did: not only to give correct answers, either, but also to challenge the teacher's lectures if she didn't agree with them.

She was a puzzle to Glenn. Most of his friends, himself included, went to school because they had to, but Caroline acted as if she really chose to be there. And even though her favorite subject was English, she held a special place in her heart for science. Not because she liked it, but because it didn't come naturally to her.

"Why would you like Science if you're not good at it?" he had once asked.

"Because it's a challenge for me to overcome. How difficult is it to get A's in the subjects I'm good at? I think it's much more admirable to excel in the ones I like the least."

Unbeknownst to her, getting an A in Science was going to be more difficult than she could imagine due to the teacher's obvious distaste for Caroline and her endless questions. Everyone quickly realized the Science teacher found the new girl's intellectual curiosity more threatening than charming.

He would never forget that day in Science class. Mr. Leeds was sidetracked as usual, disregarding the planned lesson on balancing chemical equations and instead lecturing on the Creation theory. To Glenn, the entire concept was old news, boring verses gleaned from the Bible made to sound like they came from a science textbook. He had attended enough Sunday School classes to know the whole God-created-the-world-in-six-days-and-then-he-rested-on-the-seventh. Until that day in class, he never questioned the story. But Caroline, the true skeptic, raised her hand. Even before she spoke, Glenn had a feeling the teacher wasn't going to like her question. He was right.

"Mr. Leeds, how can we be so sure those were actual days? I've been reading articles that would contradict your theory."

Mr. Leeds spun around and fastened his eyes on her. "Miss Richards," he seethed, "Your classmates may get a chuckle out of your decision to challenge my authority – no, I take that back – challenge God's authority, but I find your questions disrespectful, heretical, and utterly baseless! Now, I suggest you reread your Bible, pray to God that He forgives you for your ignorance, and keep those despicable questions to yourself."

The teacher marched over to Caroline's desk and leaned over until his face was inches from hers. "Better yet, Miss Richards, try to figure out a way to stop the Devil from entering that pretty little head of yours and filling it with such doubt. My goodness, we wouldn't want to have a doubting Caroline along with Doubting Thomas, would we?" He straightened and looked at the rest of the class. "You do remember him from the Bible, don't you? Look at how his life turned out, what with those spears being thrown at him…" Mr. Leeds chuckled at his poor excuse for a joke.

Her face turned red, but in true Caroline style, she refused to lower her head in shame. It was in that instant that Glenn knew he was completely, truly in love with this girl. What audacity she had! What openmindedness! It wasn't out of rebellion that she questioned things, he realized. It was a true love of learning that drove Caroline. He had never known anyone quite like her. Yes, Caroline had opened his eyes to a world that Glenn never knew existed, and when she accepted his shy offer to catch a movie together, he thought he must be the luckiest guy in the world.

But luck always has a way of running out.

CHAPTER 9

A Sign

LILLIAN

Lillian waved goodbye to the other members of the support group as she drove out of the parking lot. Thoughts spun in her head like a lazy daydream as she drove home from the Community Center.

Lillian parked the car in the garage and looked at the hood again. *It's dented, but I'm the one who's really broken.*

Her stomach tightened with each step toward the phone. Walking slowly through the hall, she prayed: *Please, no phone messages from Paul!* She exhaled deeply: the phone displayed, *Messages: 0.*

With a renewed sense of hope, she walked over to the freezer and pulled out a half-gallon of Chunky Monkey. *If I keep using Ben and Jerry's as a reward for No-Paul-Calls,* I'm *going to be the Chunky Monkey!* She smiled at the thought yet simultaneously felt the button on her recently-too-tight jeans digging into her stomach.

Oh well, she thought, *God won't hate me for being a few pounds over-weight. And isn't that what really matters?*

The self-talk didn't completely convince her, but she was trying. She had to try: Radio Rev's sermons emphasized getting it right, because getting it wrong would mean Eternal Punishment. Though all of this was new to her, she knew she couldn't make a mistake. If she could just be perfect, she could elude that Eternal Punishment she didn't even want to think about!

Lillian sat at the kitchen table, deep in thought while shoveling the ice cream into her mouth. She almost dropped the spoon when the phone trilled. The calm, cool feeling disappeared, replaced by a tight sensation in the pit of her stomach. *Paul.*

Do I answer it? She looked at the clock. 10:00 PM. The same time he rang last night, and that conversation continued into the wee hours of the morning. *I can't do this again. I just can't.*

C'mon, Lil, she coached herself. *Be strong and let the machine pick up. You don't need another sleepless night. If you cave in, you're one step closer to letting Paul creep back into your life.*

She held the edge of the table with both hands, willing herself to remain in the chair and ignore the call. There was a pause and then silence. She held her breath. *Will he try to call back?*

She waited one minute, then two, then three. After ten minutes, she released her grip on the table and walked over to the answering machine, where the blinking light indicated that the caller left a message. Just before she pressed the play button, she pulled her hand back as if the phone were burning hot.

Don't listen to the message tonight. Go to bed, sleep well, and then listen to it in the morning when you're less emotional. You're not ready for Paul tonight. Let it go.

She kept talking to herself as if she were the counselor talking to the patient. She walked upstairs and changed into her nightgown. Slowly, she lowered herself onto her side of the bed, the side she always slept on when Paul had been there, and the side she continued to sleep on now. Too tired to kneel, she began her prayers as her head touched the pillow, but the words floated off into oblivion as she drifted into a heavy sleep.

A SIGN

As Lillian slept, the doorknob turned, and the front door opened slowly. A shadowy figure pushed its way into the foyer of the tiny house and moved down the hall, into the kitchen, stopping in the center of the room.

The gloved hands unscrewed the light fixture. The same hands inserted a small device inside. The shoulders bobbed up and down a few times with laughter, and the hands continued their work, as if they had done this a hundred times before.

After reassembling the fixture, he gingerly slid the screwdriver into the black leather jacket pocket. He looked at his handiwork. *No one would ever notice a difference.*

The shadow slithered back towards the front door. He paused and contemplated climbing the stairs. He put one foot on the bottom step.

Nah, I need to do my research and then decide how to handle the situation. "Fixing" the light is what I came for. Nothing else. He breathed into the ski mask. The smell of whiskey filled his nostrils.

Time to go home. Looking around at the familiar wood floor and slightly dusty end tables, he wondered, *But where is home?*

He glanced up the stairs once again. *It's supposed to be here. She's the one who ruined it, but it won't be long until it's my home again. I just need to be patient – and wait. Soon enough, I'll know what to do.*

Yet again, he tried to reassure himself: *This will be a new beginning, not the end. My plan will be perfect! Just perfect.*

CHAPTER 10

Reassurance

HOPE

My phone rang, and I answered it before my mom could tell me I should be studying English instead of talking to Karen.

"Hey," Karen breathed. "What're you up to?"

I looked at the dance flyer and thought of Maddie Braun and her charmed life. "Not much," I lied. "What's up?"

"Just wanted to make sure we had a ride to the dance. My parents will be gone, so are you sure your mom can drive us? And I found out today that Anthony is definitely going. His first dance this year! Do you think it's a sign? Like, maybe he knows I'll be there, so now he wants to go?"

I smiled and decided not to be surprised or annoyed that Karen wanted to talk about Anthony – again. I indulged her for a half hour, reassuring her that my mom's gas tank was full and ready to drive us Friday night.

She paused before we hung up. "Oh, Hope? By the way, is Eli going to be there?"

She finally remembered that Hope Minor has a life, too. "I dunno. But I hope so!"

CHAPTER 11

Looking for Love

RADIO REV

All good things must come to an end, Glenn soon realized. By November of that year, Caroline was talking about going North for College. Vassar, Brown, Princeton – all these prestigious names rolled off her tongue simply, but he knew their life as a couple was going to get complicated very quickly. With his father's meager salary, Glenn's family would be lucky to afford tuition at the local community college, much less at some high-priced, out-of-state university.

How he wished he could go to a college neighboring Caroline's school! Of course, the ultimate would be to go to the same school, but even he was smart enough to know that his average grades weren't going to grant him access to elite institutions.

Caroline was different, though. She actually had a chance. Plus, she was smart enough, poor enough, and well-rounded enough to be a prime scholarship candidate. And if her brains weren't enough, years of volunteerism and varsity letters in soccer and track completed the perfect resume for any school, Ivy League or no. Though unheard of, she was accepted at all three of her college choices, but she chose the one that offered her the free ride – Princeton.

Glenn tried to be happy for her, but secretly his heart was breaking. What he lacked in intelligence he made up for in street smarts. He knew that once Caroline got exposed to true academia, there was no way he could compete. Sure, she may still be fond of Glenn in a first love kind of way, but he knew it was only a matter of time before he would get the *I just want to be friends* speech. He could almost picture her strolling by massive brick buildings, hand in hand with some preppy Tad or Dixon or Montgomery.

A warrior on the football field but an insecure creature when it came to girls, Glenn decided to be proactive. Rather than wait for the inevitable ending to this tragic tale, he would make it short and sweet. Plus, he liked being in control, so if he couldn't predict what Caroline might do in the future, he could control her ability to break up with him. He would beat her to it.

⋙◆⋘

He shook his head and tried to clear the memories from his mind. *Focus! Focus, I say! That was years ago, and you need to be in control of yourself. This revival is a big deal...everyone at home will be listening in, and rooting for you!* The tingling anticipation filled his veins, knowing that the sister station in Georgia was going to air the revival. His family would finally be able to tune in for this broadcast.

Then, he heard it: *God knows.*

There it was – again. That still, small voice that popped up at the most inopportune times. It was that voice that doubted his radio message, week after week. It was that voice that disagreed with his methods to get new listeners – and donations. It was that voice that kept reminding him he was a grown-up and didn't need his parents' approval.

God knows what you're doing.

He shook his head again. *Enough of this nonsense! I'm letting memories cloud my sense of reason and better judgment. Focus. Focus. Focus....*

HOPE

I tried to focus, but it was too boring. I looked at the clock, willing the minute hand to speed up. Ms. Tievel droned on about how the author was writing about a chair that wasn't just a chair, but a symbol for something else. *Why can't a chair just be a chair?* I thought.

After another look at the ancient clock above the chalkboard, I wondered, *How many other students have looked at this same clock over the years?* Now even the second hand crawled. In three minutes, though, the weekend would officially begin.

First, Karen and I were going to walk to her house after school and get ready for the dance, since there were more flat irons, hair dryers, and nail polish at the Pandora's than at a salon. Then, my mom would drive us to the dance.

I sighed with anticipation. Maybe Eli would be there. Even though most juniors didn't go – they're too cool for dances in the gym, I guess – there was a part of me that hoped that he was serious when he mentioned it a few days ago.

After years of doing my best to ignore Pat's friends, I suddenly noticed that one of them didn't seem quite so annoying anymore. Now, instead of heading for my room when the boys came knocking for my brother, I began lingering in the kitchen – just a little. But only when Eli was over. And then, one day, it happened. Eli popped into the room for a drink of water, without my brother.

"Where's Pat?" I had asked.

"Outside, I guess," Eli had mumbled. His dark hair was slightly messy from playing football, but I found it incredibly cute. He smiled as if he were embarrassed.

Why didn't I ever notice those white teeth before?

I stammered, "Oh. Want some Gatorade?"

As usual, I wished I had something more interesting to say, especially in light of the fact that he already had a glass of water. But Eli didn't seem to mind. Ignoring his polite "No, thanks," I poured the blue juice into a glass anyway and thought, *Now I know how Karen feels when she's around Anthony.*

Just yesterday, Eli had sauntered into the kitchen again, grinning. I jumped when I realized who it was, hoping he didn't notice my shaking hands. I thought back to Chapter Two in *Finding Your Voice: Take a risk. Do it today!*

"Hey," I said casually "What's up?"

He ran his hand over the back of his head, as if he were commanding his wispy hair to behave and lay flat. For a moment, I wondered if Eli felt as uncomfortable as I did. He coughed and said, "Umm, I was just wondering if you're going to the dance on Friday…"

His voice trailed off in a crackle. *Is it nerves?*

I tried to stop the churning of my stomach and the thoughts that spun through my head like some mental spin cycle. Somehow I managed to utter a relatively coherent answer. I nodded my head. "I think I'll be there. Why?"

Now Eli was visibly squirming. *Because of me?* I wondered incredulously. I never thought someone as cute as Eli – especially someone two years older! – would express an interest in me.

He said, "I dunno. Just asking. Maybe I'll see you there." With that, he gave me what looked like a wink as he backed out of the room.

I called after him, "Okay. See ya!"

Once my breathing returned to normal, I considered the conversation. That's when the thought hit me: *maybe he wasn't winking. Maybe he had something in his eye!*

Despite my doubts, I decided that if Eli really did wink at me, then that was definitely a sign of more good things to come! I sighed and felt that familiar tingling feeling that surfaced whenever I thought about Eli and his bright smile.

Somewhere in the back of my mind a humming noise interrupted my daydream. It was Ms. Tievel's voice. "Please remember to study all of the symbolism in the novel, especially the scene with the chair. Test Monday!"

We groaned at the prospect of weekend homework. Ms. Tievel was the only teacher who insisted on giving homework on Fridays and tests on Mondays.

I guess I can study tomorrow. After Karen sleeps over, I'll have nothing to do for the rest of the weekend, anyway.

CHAPTER 12

The Voice

RADIO REV

Friday Afternoon

Time to go home. He stepped out into the sunshine and put a hand over his eyes at the sudden brightness. He swallowed, and felt the beginning of a sore throat. *Not now. Not this weekend…*

Driving home, he thought about his secret to success. Parking the car, he wondered where he would be without the secret. Walking into his study, he knew with certainty that the secret was the reason the revival would attract unheard of amounts of money.

Over time, he simply called the secret The Voice. He discovered The Voice about six months into working with Suzanne, when he had mindlessly clicked on an internet article about mind reform. Intrigued, Glenn read the article about how people throughout history had used certain techniques to control a person's mental state, even against the person's will.

The part that really caught his attention was the final paragraph: "Some tightly-knit organizations, including religious groups, have used these techniques with dramatic results. This research reinforces yet again that the mind is a highly suggestible organ that can be molded in almost any direction, depending on the controller's motives."

He sat with those words for a few minutes. "Power of the human mind…"

My father was a good man, with pure intentions. He definitely used some of those techniques, but I never considered it mind control. That's like brainwashing, right?

Images of war prisoners being tormented by enemy soldiers competed with fond memories of his father at the pulpit.

If Dad used any of those techniques, even unknowingly, it was certainly for good – wasn't it? Using a few of these ideas wouldn't be like serious brainwashing… right?

A bolt of inspiration warmed his whole body with possibility. *What if I used some of those ideas – but only for good?*

Sure, WFAM had been doing well financially since he started preaching there, but how about those other evangelists with those mega-churches? *What's their secret?*

Ignoring the warning signs in his head, he continued researching, continued telling himself that influencing people's thoughts can be a positive thing. That if he were to turn people to God, the ends would justify the means. That people who used mind reform to hurt people were the ones who were doing the real brainwashing. That wouldn't be him.

And that was how The Voice began. He learned about the voice roll, a technique that could send the listener's brainwaves into a state where he or she would accept the speaker's words and ideas without question. After hours of practice, he decided to give it a go during the taping. Glenn had arrived in the recording room early that day, ready as ever. As he preached, he found the speaking speed easy to maintain, almost effortless. *I must be a natural!*

When the tapes with The Voice aired the following week, the response was nothing short of amazing. Suzanne even called to share the news, and he knew her call must be an emergency – he made it crystal clear that a true emergency was the only circumstance under which he should be interrupted at home.

"Hello?"

"Rev, you won't believe this!"

"Suzanne, is that you?" *This better be good.*

"Oh, yeah. Sorry! Anyway, I just *had* to call to let you know that your broadcasts this week have doubled our donations! I don't know what you did, but it's pure genius!"

Suzanne paused, and Rev remained silent. *The Voice actually worked?*

"RR? You still there?"

Glenn could barely think straight, yet he managed a confused, "That's terrific, Suzanne. Thank you for – "

She cut him off. "But that's not the best part! There's a buzz going around that you might get some sort of bonus for this. Imagine that! WFAM – giving out bonuses? It's insane!"

And without waiting for his reaction, Suzanne continued yammering away, oblivious to the one-sidedness of the conversation. Five minutes into her soliloquy, she paused.

"Oops, gotta go, Rev. Someone else is calling in. Probably more donations! Bye…"

Glenn sat in stunned silence, holding the phone in his hand long after Suzanne hung up. *It worked.* A mere experiment had proven to be more powerful than he could fathom in a single week.

Clearly, he had tapped into a resource with infinite possibilities. The entire time, a very small, but very insistent part of him whispered, *You're brainwashing them.*

"Noooo!" he shouted to the empty room in response to the memory. He banged his fist on the desk, sending a flurry of papers to the floor. Whenever his conscience reared its ugly head, he fought it, just like he fought off defenders on opposing football teams years before. He was good at fighting back, and he liked to win. Even against himself.

He reached into the desk drawer, took out a piece of paper, and wrote:

The Good That Has Come from The Voice...

1. Teaching others about God

2. More money for WFAM (and me)

3. Making my parents proud

4. Making my family and friends proud

5. Forgetting Caroline

He looked over the list. As much as he hated to admit it, he realized that only the first item on the list actually helped others. Every other idea helped one person, and one person only – him. He crumpled up the paper and tossed it in the direction of the wastebasket on the other side of his office.

He missed.

CHAPTER 13

Dancing with the Devil

HOPE

Friday 7:30 PM

Karen scanned the crowd in the parking lot and elbowed me in the ribs. "Ouch!"

She ignored my comment and whispered, "Look! There's Anthony. Let's go say hi."

"Saying hi" was Karen's code for joining Anthony and his friends and scoring the ultimate goal later: getting together with him for the one and only "slow dance." At every Roosevelt dance, the deejay ends the evening with the same speech: "Okay, folks, we're gonna slow things down a little. So grab a sweetie and get out on the floor!"

Even though everyone groans about "grabbing a sweetie" (how old is this guy, anyway?), we still do what he says. And after three months of looking over the shoulder of whoever I was dancing with, I've developed a theory. There's only a single slow song for one reason, and one reason only: the teachers can't stand being on red alert to prevent all the groping and grinding that's inevitable. I mean, face it – the slow dance is your opportunity to show the person you've been obsessed with that you care.

Picture this: the teachers circulate madly through the crowd of couples, tapping on the shoulders of the ones who are not simply dancing but grinding up against one another and then pulling apart the really brazen ones who are totally hooking up. By the end of those three minutes (which can be like heaven, if you get to dance with the right person!), Principal Vambles is practically pushing us out the door, more than ready to release us and our hormones into our parents' idling cars.

Karen and I threaded our way through the thick scent of aftershave and perfume until we found Anthony and his three reliable sidekicks – Brandon, Robert, and Carlos. Anthony took center stage.

"Listen to this! You're not gonna believe it! Remember what I told ya about Miss Lillian's church in her house?" The six of us nodded. "Now things are getting even weirder. I was walking by the teacher's lunch room, and Miss Lillian was in there talking. You know how she talks real loud?" We nodded again, this time a little more impatiently, wondering when he was going to get to the good part.

"Well, she was saying things like…" He raised his voice in a mock-woman's tone: "'He's out of control! He's insane! He won't leave me alone, and I swear he was listening in on my phone calls, because whenever I talk to him, he seems to know about every phone conversation I've had. How can that even be? He's lives across town now.'"

My eyes widened with every sentence of his far-fetched story. This was a little bit too unbelievable, even for Anthony — the female version of Karen in the exaggeration department.

Karen stopped him. "Wait a minute…how did you hear all this without her noticing you?"

"I just took a reeeeeal long drink at the water fountain next to the door." He grinned mischievously. His voice sounded innocent. "You know, I'm an athlete who gets thirsty! At least, that was what I was gonna say if anyone noticed. But wait, guys! That's not even the good part!" He stopped again, making sure we were all listening. We were.

Anthony lowered his voice to a stage whisper. "After a few minutes, she said something like, 'If I didn't know him better, I would be scared for my life!'"

I shook my head, as if that would clear away the cloud of unsettling thoughts. "Anthony, that's just whacked out. This town's idea of crime is a missing cat! You want us to believe there's some madman on the loose?"

"I know, I know, I could hardly believe it myself! That's why I eavesdropped for so long. That, and I didn't want to go back to English class. Y'know, Ms. Tievel can't take a joke about anything! It's all read, read, read, and write, write, write, with her shrivelly old face and fish lips ready to yell at one of us for doing nothing!"

I tried to help him refocus. "Was that all Miss Lillian said?"

Anthony turned to face me. He barked, "No! There's more, if you would just let me finish!"

Everyone, except for puppy-dog Karen, rolled their eyes at him. He took the hint, and talked faster. "I'm tellin' ya, it's all too strange! The whole thing ended with her saying that she has this church in her basement, and it would be such a shame if psycho-guy came in the house because he'd probably destroy all her hard work."

Karen gasped, "She called him 'psycho-guy'?"

Anthony smiled. "No, I forget his name. Pete, or Paul, maybe? I dunno. That's just what I'm calling him. Hey, if the name fits…"

Karen's eyes were glued on Anthony. Not only was this her crush, but he seemed to have the best news scoop to ever hit Roosevelt High!

"And?" Karen asked. I could almost imagine her scribbling story details in that mind of hers. See, Karen has a photographic memory, so where most people need to write everything down to remember, Karen will just file away the information with a lot of head nodding, and voila! It's like someone typed a transcript of the conversation in her mind. It was amazing, and I knew if she really wanted to be a news anchor, her dream would come true someday.

I spoke up again. "Is that it?"

Anthony narrowed his eyes. "What do you mean, 'Is that it?' What I told you isn't enough?"

I shrugged while Anthony added, "Yeah, that's it, but think about everything she said – she's got a church – in her basement? There's a crazed lunatic spying on her, and she's afraid for her life because of this guy? And don't forget the one-eighty she did in personality, too!"

"I totally agree," Karen said. "It's absolutely bizarre, but how do the crazy guy, a personality change, and the church fit together? I don't get it."

"Me neither," Anthony said. "Who knows? Maybe Miss Lillian will come to the dance and we can see if the axe murderer is following her!" He approached Karen from behind and circled one arm around her waist. With his free hand, he held an imaginary knife to her throat. Everyone laughed, except for Karen, who looked like she was about to faint from his nearness.

Principal Vambles brought us back to reality. "OK, Ladies and Gentlemen! Listen up, and no one will get hurt…" All the kids groaned as Mr. Vambles laughed at his own idea of a joke. With his poor sense of comedic timing, most adults find nothing scary about the man. But, we students knew there was something secretive and dark in his shark-like eyes. Even the most hardened bullies at school were careful around our principal.

Mr. Vambles directed, "Please file into the gymnasium, single-file. Single-file, I said! Did you hear that, Mr. Gerome?" Nate Gerome, one of the bullies who tried to act innocent around Mr. Vambles, clearly couldn't fool the principal, who seemed know that Nate's good behavior switched on and off like a light.

We filed into the Vambles-mandated single-file line behind Maddie and Krystal. The two queen bees marched into the dance, noses in the air, waving to the popular boys and turning their backs on people like Danny Zolor, my neighbor. *How rude!* I thought.

Krystal and Maddie had sized up Danny back in September, and they haven't been anything other than nasty to him since then. Even though he's a freshman like us, Danny should be a sophomore. An extra year in first grade sealed his fate, and Danny was, by far, our most mature-looking classmate, with a deep voice and the hint of a moustache. Unfortunately, the extra year didn't help him catch up with his learning. Even though I've never liked Danny like *that,* I knew he was one of the sweetest guys in our school.

Watching Krystal and Maddie brush past him as if they didn't even know him made my blood boil. They certainly acted like they knew him in Science class earlier that day! Everyone could see his crumpled test sticking out of his notebook with the bright red *F* at the top. It was the safety test we had just taken in Science class that our teacher said would be our easy A. All we had to do was use our notes (yes, it was open book) to answer the ten questions. Most questions were ridiculously simple, like, "True or false: when you turn on the Bunsen burner, try to lean over it and let your hair touch the flames." Or, "Fill in the blank: The red fire extinguisher should be used to put out a _____ (hint: it begins with the letter F).

I felt horrible for Danny. How could he have failed that test? Once I heard someone say he has a processing disorder (which I know nothing about), but I do know that his disability spells disaster for him, especially in the presence of Maddie and Krystal. Wishing madly that the girls wouldn't see the test, I cringed when their comments unfolded like the script to a bad play:

KRYSTAL: Ooh, Danny, I think your backpack is unzipped.

MADDIE: Let me help.

DANNY (confused): Oh, well, OK.

KRYSTAL: Danny, you've got a test here, did you know that?

DANNY: Uhh…

MADDIE: It looks like the science test. (Pause.) It is the science test! (Mock horror.) Oh, no! It says F, Danny! Did you see that?

KRYSTAL (in the loudest voice possible): I'm so sorry to hear you got an F on that test. Don't worry; it'll be our little secret.

DANNY (looking confused and stunned): Uhh, yeah. OK.

As we walked out of class, Danny leaned over and whispered to me, "Hope, they said they'll keep it a secret, so why did Krystal say it so loud?"

I looked at his face and could see that he was truly puzzled. I couldn't bear to give him the harsh truth, so I just said, "I'm sure they'll keep it a secret. I guess Krystal doesn't know how loud her voice gets." I had to bite the inside of my mouth to prevent myself from telling Danny what I really thought of Krystal and Maddie.

"Yeah, you're probably right. I mean, how could such a pretty girl do something mean?" He gave a nervous chuckle and looked at me expectantly.

I played the game – sort of. "Well, just because someone's pretty, it doesn't mean their personality matches." I instantly regretted what I said when I saw Danny's confused expression. "Don't worry, Danny. All I'm saying is, try to get to know people for personality, not looks." *Now I sound really parental.*

"You mean like Miss Lillian? She's got an awesome personality. That's the first thing I noticed about her! I like her whistling, too!"

Once again, Danny was a day late and a dollar short. He obviously hadn't noticed the personality change in Miss Lillian, but I didn't dare correct him again and confuse him further. "Yeah, just like Miss Lillian, Danny. Just like that."

When we were safely out of the principal's earshot, I asked, "Kar, do you think Miss Lillian will be here? She's already stopped the office singing. Don't you think dancing might be next?"

Except for slow dance time, most teachers who chaperoned Roosevelt dances hovered on the edge of the gym, making sure the freshman boys didn't run around and try to tackle people who were actually attempting to dance. Miss Lillian was different, though. She talked to us and even danced at times!

"Good insight, Hope. See? You think you're not cut out for reporting, but you're great at taking in all the information and putting together the pieces that don't quite fit. Kind of like seeing the outliers from our graphs in math. You see the outliers in people and stories."

I smiled. One thing I loved about Karen is that, while she tries to get her way by sweet-talking me, she really is genuine with her compliments. I knew this was her way of making another pitch for us to become co-journalists.

Karen continued, "Let's get into that gym and find the mysterious secretary." She switched over to her newscaster voice, which is a little deeper than her normal tone. "Is Miss Lillian, one of the most dependable chaperones at Roosevelt High School, truly a changed woman? Will she never dance – or whistle – again? Let's find out."

RADIO REV

Friday 7:30 PM

Glenn walked away from his animated colleagues and retreated to his office for a few minutes of solitude. *How is it that my "day job" requires evening hours every month?*

He looked at the revival paperwork on his desk, reading the material over and over. Nothing was sinking in. He was too far into his overplayed memory to stop now. It felt more like high school again as he remembered that fateful day.

It was senior year, and Caroline and Glenn were sitting on his front porch, sipping lemonade. Caroline mused, "I still don't understand what Mr. Leeds has against me. I mean, don't teachers want students to participate and ask thoughtful questions?" She looked truly puzzled.

Glenn made up his mind. This was his opening, and he took it. "Do you want to know the truth? Wanna know what I really think?"

Even as he said the words, it pained him. He knew he didn't want to do this, but he knew with equal certainty that he didn't want to be heartbroken a year from now, when he would be even more in love with this girl than he was at the moment.

Caroline glanced sideways at him. "Yes, of course! Of course I want to know what you think. What is it?"

Glenn looked at those bright blue eyes and shuddered as the words passed from his lips. "The problem is, you think you're better than all of us in this town, and you use your questions to put us down. We all go to the same church – including you! – and we all know the answers to the Creation question. It's what we've been taught, and that's never gonna change." *Man, this is hard to do, especially when I'm not really upset with her!*

Caroline didn't respond at first, as if his words refused to sink in. During that slight pause, Glenn saw her raise her shoulders and take a deep breath. He knew her so well. This was her way of preparing herself to say something difficult. Glenn had never been on the receiving end of Caroline after the shoulder-raise.

"Glenn, I don't know what's gotten into you lately! Ever since you helped me mail off those college applications, you've been moping around with sad puppy-dog eyes. Usually, when I ask a question like the one I asked Mr. Leeds, you tell me how you love my bravery and intelligence. But the past few weeks you haven't said that. In fact, it looks like my questions hurt you somehow. This has nothing to do with you! If I don't ask, how will I ever learn? How will I grow? How will I find the answers to my questions? I thought you, of all people, understood that."

Glenn cast his eyes down at his ratty sneakers as Caroline continued her rant. He did understand, but to admit that would mean future heartbreak for him. Of that Glenn was sure.

"You always said that you hated being the preacher's son, that everyone had all these unreasonable expectations of you. Like you had to be perfect or something. I've never asked you to be perfect, have I? Have I ever judged you for the times you told me what you really thought about your family? Your church? The people of this town? And now you're going to give me that kind of answer? How could you? You know that you've questioned things, too. You told me that last year! Why the change now?"

She was right. Since they started dating, he found Caroline to be the warmest, most accepting person he'd ever met. Ever. And he had questioned some of his beliefs, but he knew he could never ask his parents about it. They just wouldn't understand.

So now, the time had arrived: the moment of truth. Would he take the risk? Risk having his heart broken? Or, would he play it safe? Be the good son, and forget about Caroline, her infectious smile, her incredible questions?

He knew how his parents felt about Caroline. Of course, they never outright said they didn't like her. No, that wouldn't be the Christian thing to do. But he could tell what they really thought of her by the disapproving expression on his mother's face and by his father's silence whenever Caroline's name was mentioned.

At the beginning of their relationship, their opinions hadn't mattered much. He was so smitten with Caroline that he ignored the uncomfortable silences and raised eyebrows. But now that college loomed closer, the more alone he felt.

He'd be back home, without her. He would still be surrounded by the guilt that he wasn't pleasing his parents. His friends and family would be his only support network, and even his friends weren't supportive anymore. They were tired of trying to include him and Caroline in their plans, only to meet with disapproving friends' parents who didn't trust anyone who didn't fit into the Mountwell mold.

Admittedly, the free-thinking Caroline triggered suspicion among his parents and peers, but her motives were pure. What you saw was what you got with Caroline. *The truly innocent one of the bunch is the black sheep.* Whenever Glenn saw the loving reception his friends' girlfriends would get from his parents, he felt an anger rising in him that he had never known before.

And yet… family was family. Try as he might to pretend it didn't matter, as much as he tried to be the typical rebellious teen, there was a tiny part of Glenn that couldn't completely shake their disapproval.

Caroline repeated herself. "So, Glennie, what is it? Why have you been so irritable lately?"

He thought carefully about his response. Had he changed? Why was he being so argumentative? She at least deserved an answer to her question about Mr. Leeds.

After a few moments, he was ready. He made his choice and swallowed hard. As he opened his mouth to answer her, he knew he had reached the point of no return.

PAUL

Friday 7:30 PM

He pushed "Play" on the recording device and listened to the conversation for the tenth time – just to be sure he didn't miss any key information. The recorder picked up only one phone conversation that week, but what he heard gave him more questions than answers.

"Hi. My name is 'Lil' Lady,' and I'd like to enter to win the two tickets." Pause. "Oh, which contest? The contest for the Radio Rev Revival Weekend. "

Another pause. "Mhmm. You're sure? All the tickets have been sold out?" *Was that disappointment in her voice?* "Oh, really? You still have tickets for the sunrise service?"

Lillian shrieked, and Paul jumped, even though he'd heard the recording nine times before. "There's no fee? Really? Why are the other ones so expensive and this one's free?"

A giggle followed the silence. "Hmmm. Well, their loss is my gain!"

Paul grimaced as Lillian gushed, "I didn't think I'd be able to afford to go unless I won, so this is too good to be true! To actually see and meet Radio Rev..."

A final pause, and then, "Oh, I see. I'll get to hear him but not see him? That's okay with me. Wow, I've been calling and calling, and to know at the last minute that I can go....I feel like Cinderella going to the ball! Woo-hoo!"

Woo-hoo? Cinderella? And why does my wife want to see this person? Radio Rev? What kind of name is that? It can't be a real reverend... Lil's not a church gal. Never was, anyway. Although, she has been saying "prayer" an awful lot and talking about souls.

Paul allowed the rational side of his brain to argue, *No, it's probably some guy she's trying to meet now that I've been banished from the house. My house. My life.*

The familiar feeling of heat rose in his chest. He grabbed the cold can from the nightstand and gulped, as if that would wash away the rush of hate-inducing emotions. He snarled, "What is it they say?" In a sing-song voice he cried, "The definition of insanity is doing the same thing over and over and expecting different results. Well, then, I guess I'm insane for picking up this drink like I always do. But, at least I'm insane *and* drunk!"

He staggered over to the small mirror above the sink and laughed at his sallow complexion. "What a place! It's so cozy that I can eat, sleep, and take a piss without walking more than five steps!"

Just as quickly as the alcohol could make him laugh, it could lead him to fits of rage that even he couldn't understand. The fire in his chest refused to go away. Mentally, he admonished his reflection with facts.

I'm Paul Amadon, top salesman at Unicorp. I've been successful all my life: first, All-State football champion at Octomara High School, then All-State linebacker for Gettysbury College. Girls always loved me, and women still do! Sure, I like to unwind after work with a drink – or two – but who doesn't want to relax after a hard day at the office? I married my college sweetheart, and she still loves me.

He glared at himself again, daring this pathetic-looking image to fight back. Paul screamed at himself: "Oh, you think just because I'm in this shithole that Lillian doesn't love me? Well, mister, you've got another thing coming to you! She does love me! She does….she does…."

Anyone observing Paul at that moment would have noticed that his eyes had changed, shifted in an almost imperceptible way. Instead of the sad, sometimes angry expression that stared back at him so many nights since Lillian kicked him out, his eyes now lacked any human emotion. They were black. Vacant. Void.

"She does love me…she does…" he repeated. He walked over to the tiny excuse for a closet. He opened the door, reached up on the top shelf and cradled the black, shiny object in his hand. Carefully, he wrapped it in a handkerchief.

Putting the bulging handkerchief in his back pocket, he grabbed his keys in one hand, and the silver can in the other. With a few quick gulps, the beer was gone.

He looked at his watch. *Sports-N-More, and time for a few more,* he rhymed. *I've got plenty of time to pay Lillian a little visit before that sunrise service of hers.*

CHAPTER 14

Her Song

HOPE

Friday 8:45 PM

Two teachers were DJ-ing and actually playing decent songs. Several girls had formed a circle and were dancing in a way that was definitely not what Mr. Vambles would consider "school-appropriate", but the other teachers didn't seem to notice.

Nate Gerome and his posse were trying to see who could shove the most pizza in his mouth at once. Sauce was dripping all over their T-Shirts, but they didn't care. These guys definitely weren't here to make a good impression on girls, and the messier, the more cheers they received. Nate looked like a chipmunk with cheese dripping from his lips, and his best friend, Mark, was throwing cola-covered ice cubes from his soda at anyone walking by. We quickly passed that group so as not to get pelted with ice and inched towards the side of the gym. That's where most of our friends hung out, taking in the scene, and trying not to look awkward, even though we were all feeling totally self-conscious.

I scanned the room, hoping to see Eli. Nothing. The little knot of anticipation in my stomach tightened at the thought that he may not arrive. *Maybe he's too mature for this kind of thing. I mean, he's a junior. What does he want with a bunch of freshmen? Or a girl like me?*

I caught a glimpse of a long sleeved shirt and grabbed Karen's hand. "There she is! Pretty plain for a dance, but she's here!"

Karen looked and nodded as her eyes fixed on Miss Lillian. "But look at how she's standing there. The live mannequins at the mall can't even stand that still. And...omigod! They're playing her song."

Earlier in the year, kids dubbed any song from the 80's or 90's as "Miss Lillian's song". We had noticed that the teachers would go up to the DJs and make requests. Inevitably, he would grant one of their requests, so we were guaranteed to be forced to listen to at least one song from Michael Jackson, Madonna, or M.C. Hammer. And then Miss Lillian and Mr. Tullo would dance.

I think that Mr. Tullo, the gym teacher, missed his calling as a street performer, because whenever "her song" comes on, the kids form a circle around him. He'll do all these eighties-style break dancing moves, including the worm, handstands, and once, a backflip. All the while, the kids chant, "Go Tullo, go Tullo! Go, go, go Tullo!" and Miss Lillian stands off to the side, waiting for her turn.

When Mr. Tullo gets tired, he points to Miss Lillian, and she struts towards the inside of the circle. Then, she starts dancing like a robot, which is pretty funny to see, considering she's a middle-aged lady. At that point, Mr. Tullo rallies the kids to change the chant to, "Miss Lil', Miss Lil'! Miss, Miss, Miss Lil'!" Even though the song and dance is predictable and lame, there's something about the spectacle that draws us in every time.

Tonight, Miss Lillian appeared robot-move-less. Mr. Tullo was already in motion, spinning around on the floor – were those his feet in the air? – but the dance regulars knew what was in store for part two, so they were trying to find the second dancer.

I looked at Miss Lillian again. She stood at the gym door, frozen, a pained look on her face. The only thing moving were her hands, which looked as if they were trying to pull the too-long sleeves down even further over her wrists. Karen started walking in her direction. "What are you doing?" I yelled over the pulsing music.

She stopped and turned to face me. "I'm gonna tell her it's her turn. Can you imagine how embarrassed she'll be if they're all waiting for her and she doesn't dance? Our class will never let her live it down!"

Karen was right. If there was one eternal truth about high school, it was this: one wrong move that catches the attention of a large number of students equals continued embarrassment for the next four years. No matter what the person may do from that point on, once someone's been judged harshly by the students, the impression sticks until that group graduates.

As we approached the woman, Karen joked, "Hey, Miss Lillian, time to power up! It's almost your turn!" Miss Lillian turned to face us, but her eyes looked sad and lost. After what felt like an endlessly awkward pause, she jerked her head as if shaking cobwebs from her brain so the words could register.

"Oh, Karen! And Hope! I'm sorry, girls, but I won't be dancing tonight. I'm not feeling well…." Her voice trailed off, and before we could say anything else, she fled from the gym.

Karen pulled on my hand. "C'mon, we've gotta get her to dance!" I knew Karen's stubborn look and what that meant, but I had a bad feeling. I pulled my hand back.

"I don't think this is such a good idea. Miss Lillian looks out of it, and if she's not comfortable, we're just going to make it worse!" I attempted to infuse the same urgency in my voice that Karen did when she was trying to be convincing.

She stopped for a moment, and, surprisingly, agreed with me. I should have known better, though. "You're right. Let's leave her alone.

At least, let her think we're leaving her alone." With that, Karen race-walked towards the gym doors. I followed, a new knot of anxiety forming in the pit of my stomach.

Karen must have sensed my mounting worry. She stopped in the doorway and spun around. "Let's just stroll around and see if we can catch a glimpse of our missing robot-woman." She smiled and added, "C'mon, there's nothing wrong with us walking through the hallway to get some fresh air." She fanned herself in an attempt to convince others that she was innocently cooling off. I sighed and followed her into the empty hallway. Luckily for us, the hall chaperones had entered the gym to watch Mr. Tullo's moves.

As we walked through the corridor, we heard a muffled sniffling sound. Karen put her finger over her lips – as if I were going to start talking loudly! – and backed up against the wall. I did the same, feeling like I was part of a detective movie. Bravely, Karen peeked around the corner and then jerked her head back to safety. She whispered, "Oh, shit!"

"Who is it?" I whispered back, even though I already knew the answer.

"Miss Lillian! And man, is she crying!"

I felt more uncomfortable than ever. Here we were, spying on this poor lady who obviously wanted nothing more than to be left alone. Even Karen seemed to know we had crossed the line, because she waved her hand in a gesture to follow her back into the dance. We walked slowly, as if exiting a funeral.

As we approached the gym doors, we heard a quivering voice. "Girls?" A red-eyed Miss Lillian walked towards us. My neck felt warm, and I could only imagine how red my face was turning.

Karen spoke up. "Yes, Miss Lillian?" I looked over and noticed that Karen looked completely at ease with her wide, innocent eyes and smooth speech. *How does she pull that off?* I wondered, secretly admiring her calmness under pressure.

"Would you two, umm, mind standing here for a few minutes with me? You don't have to do anything. Just kind of, you know, hang out, as they say?" She looked to us for a reaction and we both nodded and moved closer to her.

She continued, "I'll let you girls in on a little secret…"

Karen stood up ever-so-slightly. I knew that my best friend's radar was alerted by the word "secret."

Miss Lillian sighed, "I'm having a rough day, and I know that Mr. Tullo is going to be looking for me soon. He means well, but I'm just not ready for him to bother me about not doing the dance tonight. My feet weren't in the dancing mood. But if he sees you two here with me, he might not be so harsh. You both know how he can get with his kidding around, right?" She attempted a weak smile.

I knew exactly what she meant. Mr. Tullo's sarcasm wasn't lost on me, especially the day I missed the ball during our co-ed volleyball unit. "That's it, Hope," he had said, "the name of the game is 'Miss the Ball at All Costs.' Keep up the good work!"

Karen would have given the teacher a dirty look for a comment like that. But, of course, I smiled politely and pretended I didn't mind being insulted in front of my classmates. At least, I used to act that way. *Next time Tullo tries that on me, I'll give him a look he won't forget anytime soon!*

I looked up at Miss Lillian and felt pity for her. *I guess he has that embarrassing effect on everyone, including adults!*

As the woman spoke, Karen was almost drooling over the inside information, and I had to force myself not to laugh. Of course, I couldn't deny the fact that this event really did seem to have all the makings of a juicy story – drama, intrigue, and friction between two staff members.

Finally, Karen said, "We don't mind staying, Miss Lillian. In fact, I don't even think they should call these events dances: they should call them stands, since standing's all we do, anyway."

Miss Lillian laughed softly. "That's sweet of you to say, dear. You kids sure know how to cheer me up. I just say a prayer of thanks every time I get to be around you two. You brighten my day more than you realize!"

⇒◇⇐

Prayer. When Miss Lillian said that word, I remembered the last time I heard her mention prayers. It was the day after I returned to school from a horrible stomach virus (to this day, I can't stomach the thought of eating at Billy Buns Burger Factory). I had walked over to Miss Lillian's desk to give her the note Mom wrote to excuse my absence.

She was sitting in her swivel chair, deep in thought. At least, that's what it looked like until I got closer. As I approached, I could see her poring over a calendar of some sort. When she spotted me, she began firing all these crazy questions at me. Am I stressed out? Do I pray?

The whole incident creeped me out, since the only people I know who talk about praying in everyday conversation are my grandparents. But for a grandparent, it's no big deal. Face it, they're old, and lots of old people like to go to church. Here in school, though, with Miss Lillian, it seemed odd. I couldn't get out of that office fast enough, hoping she wouldn't bring it up again. Until the dance, I had almost forgotten about it. *Almost* forgotten, that is.

Now, with Miss Lillian mentioning prayers again – at a dance, no less! – Karen's idea just became a little more tempting. *Her journalistic obsession must be rubbing off on me. Now she's got me interested in this whole confusing story!*

Karen brought me back to the present with her bellowing voice and nervous laugh. Sounding like a guidance counselor, she asked, "You gonna be OK, Miss Lillian? Can we get you a soda? Or a slice of pizza?"

Miss Lillian laughed. "Oh, you're too generous! Of course I don't want you spending your money on me."

The loud music stopped briefly, and one of the deejays made an announcement. *That meant Miss Lillian was off the hook!* She must have sensed this, too, as she urged us to get back into the dance and "have a ball!"

"Wow! Awkward!" I whispered when we were out of earshot.

"I know, right? But why couldn't we keep talking to her? Try to get the scoop?"

"Be serious, Karen! What adult cries about their problems to teenagers?"

"Crazy ones with a good news story, that's who!"

I glared at her and she conceded, "Okay, it's probably time to get back inside. It's gotta be time for the slow dance!"

Walking back toward the gym, the figure before me caused my throat to tighten and my stomach to turn a somersault – Eli! Sensing that someone was behind him, he turned. When his bright eyes caught mine, I grabbed Karen to prevent myself from falling over.

He smiled – what beautiful teeth! – and drawled, "Hey, Hope. Thought maybe I missed ya…"

For once, I collected myself and answered confidently, "No, I've been here the whole time. How are you?" *Look how in control I am! That book sure is paying off…*

We talked for a few minutes, and just as I started to panic with the realization that I was running out of things to say, the deejay's voice cut through the air: "Folks, it's time to slow things down a little, so grab a sweetie and hit the floor!" The collective sigh rose through the gym, but everyone began pairing off as directed. The slow dance had begun.

I looked at Eli, who rocked back and forth on his heels. *Nerves?* I wondered.

"So, you wanna dance?"

The words refused to come out of my mouth, so I just smiled and nodded. Eli took my hand (no boy my age would be so kind!), and led me to the middle of the gym. I put my arms around his neck and felt his hands around my waist. I tried to force the dizzying feeling away, but to no avail. I threw caution to the wind and relaxed, figuring if I fainted, Eli was strong enough to catch me.

He started talking – another sign he's older and more mature…no freshmen boys actually have a conversation during the dance!

"I hope you don't mind this…"

He raised his left hand in a vague way, I guess referring to our dancing together. I just looked at him.

Eli continued, "I mean, you're my friend's little sister and all…"

I actually interrupted him! "It's okay, Eli, I'm not some little girl anymore. We're only two years apart." I smiled, trying to look equally alluring and flirtatious.

The expression must have worked, because Eli smiled again. "Yeah, I guess you're right." He leaned into me and whispered in my ear, "Besides, I don't think of you as just Pat's sister."

I glanced up and saw him wink. *So he really did wink at me the other day!*

The song was drawing to a close, and I willed the chorus to repeat a few more times. Eli must've sensed that time was almost up, because I felt his hands trail around my waist to my back. As I felt the hands move down lower and lower to the small of my back, I nervously scanned the crowd for patrolling teachers.

Luckily, the group of teachers had gathered around Maddie and Krystal's group, where a mob of partner-less boys were surrounding the girls, moving in on them like a pack of wolves who had just discovered fresh meat. Maddie and Krystal didn't seem to mind, but the teachers were scurrying around them, trying to separate the bodies unsuccessfully.

I tried to memorize every feeling, every sensation, knowing the moment couldn't last forever. Luckily, it looked like no one was going to bust us, which allowed Eli's hand to trail a little bit lower while I tried not to hyperventilate.

Eli lowered his head to my ear again, but this time instead of saying anything, I felt his lips brush against my skin. My fingers gently grazed the hair at the base of his neck, and I noticed his face turning a deep shade of red. I smiled inwardly, wanting to shout to the world, *He really likes me! This amazing boy likes ME!*

"Alright folks, time to call it a night! Be safe, have a great weekend, and we'll see you Monday!"

Mr. Vambles' voice boomed through the speakers, shocking me out of my hazy state of delirium.

Taking a deep breath, Eli exhaled slowly. "Thanks, Hope. Maybe we can, uhh, get together again, uhh, sometime soon?" His question hung in the air, waiting for my response.

I knew I was answering too quickly, maybe sounding a little bit too eager. I didn't care. "I'd like that!"

Eli didn't seem to mind my enthusiasm. "Really? How about tomorrow night? Are you busy?"

"No, I'm free." And just like that, I had a date!

We traded phone numbers, and Eli promised, "I'll text you."

I floated out of the gym, ready to burst like a balloon. For once, I would be the one with the story! For once, Karen would need to listen to me!

Karen spotted me and ran over, equally flushed and excited. "I got to dance with Anthony, and he said…" I smiled as she babbled, hearing but not really listening to her words. A reckless idea began to form in my mind as she blathered on about Anthony.

I stopped in my tracks, almost not believing what I was about to say. I guess the euphoria of the dance with Eli and the memory of his hands on my hips made me feel daring, ready for more excitement this evening.

I remembered *Finding Your Voice's* advice: *Infuse variety into your life. Be spontaneous!* I definitely needed an outlet for this inexplicable energy. Before I could talk myself out it, I burst out, "Karen, you've actually got me thinking about this whole Miss Lillian thing, and I'm reconsidering..."

Karen stopped in her tracks. She hugged me and squealed, "I knew you'd come around at some point! Miss Lillian's church basement – or whatever it is – here we come!"

I let her river of words wash over me because whenever Karen starts in on her loop, she says the same things over and over. As long as I nod every now and then, she doesn't get too angry with me for spacing out while she gushes. The river continued, "And we'll take pictures, and I'll get to meet Kurt and Missy – not like I care about meeting *that* one! – and..."

As she spoke, I tried to figure out how we were going to sneak out of my house. No matter what, my plan would need to be fool-proof. There's no way I was going to get Karen in any more trouble than she normally got herself into, and I didn't want to do anything to jeopardize my night out with Eli. I would have to think of every possible contingency.

And for once, I could do something daring. Teacher's pet Hope? Sneaking out? Spying?

I shook my head with disbelief. *I have a feeling this will be an evening I'll always remember!*

LILLIAN

Friday 8:45 PM

Lillian stepped out into the cool night, a sharp contrast from the humid, slightly sour-smelling air of Roosevelt High.

Why didn't I just do the stupid dance?

She berated herself for what seemed like the millionth time. *Then I wouldn't have had to escape, break down and cry, and have those little heathens try to make me feel better.*

Heathens, Lillian? Is that what you call them? Do you really think they're that evil?

Sometimes Lillian felt as if two people lived in her body. One was Old Lillian, the one who liked to sway with the music, whistle happy songs, and smile. That Lillian forgave and forgot. That Lillian tried to see the beauty in everyone, even someone as difficult as Paul. Poor, drunk Paul.

Then there was New Lillian, the one who was given a new life after listening to Radio Rev's rousing broadcasts. This Lillian had to check herself, second-guess all of her thoughts and actions, and then act accordingly to Radio Rev's instructions. She decided that God would not like her dancing (too worldly), or her beautiful, flowing skirts (too vain), or her open-minded thinking (too sinful).

She recalled the future world Radio Rev talked about so ominously. The time when God was going to judge the living and the dead, and not everyone would like what God had in store for the sinners. New Lillian told her to change her ways. For Lillian, that meant no more dancing.

She thought back to the day she mentioned prayer to Hope. *If I could just get her to pray…*

But Old Lillian chided, *Stop it! Hope and Karen are none of your business. Besides, who are you to judge them?*

With the car door firmly closed, she began talking to herself. Imaginary Devil and Angel returned. Knowing that no one could hear her made her feel less crazy, even though the conversation sounded like it really was taking place between two very different people.

ANGEL: "Lillian, it may be your duty to bring the girls to God, but you need to stop following Hope every day. You're on the verge of breaking the law!"

DEVIL: "But Lil, remember what Radio Rev told us the Bible says – God's law supersedes manmade laws. I'm saving Hope, so how can this be wrong?

ANGEL (with doubt): "I don't know…."

DEVIL: "Think about it. You're not going to hurt her! You're not going to torture her! You're merely going to take her to a revival to save her."

ANGEL: "But I feel guilty. I'm trailing her like a stalker!"

DEVIL (chuckling): "Stalker? Lillian, get real. Stalkers do harm. Saving someone is the most precious gift you can give someone, and gift-giving's not a crime, last time I checked!"

Lillian laughed at her own response.

She rationalized, "You're right, it's time I step up and do the right thing. Enough of this feeling guilty just because my methods don't fit into what mainstream society believes. God is happy with me, right?"

She let the question hang in the air because a small part of her avoided the answer.

As Lillian approached the first traffic light, she looked around. For the first time, she noticed a large building behind the corner convenience store. If it weren't for the tall steeple protruding into the sky with a sparkling silver cross at the top, she might not have known the building was a church.

How could I have driven down this road all these years and never seen that? The timing caused Lillian to wonder, *Is this a sign from God? Permission for what I'm about to do?*

With a deep breath, she took one last look at the church and hit the accelerator. She reached one hand up to her neck and gently touched the cross pendant that hung from a delicate silver chain.

It's time, Lillian. You can't go halfway with this any longer. It's time to be decisive. Be brave. Do what you're called to do.

Instead of turning left into her development, she made a right-hand turn into Hidden Hills. She swerved several times as she pictured snippets from her life: her long-deceased but loving parents, friends from her hometown, marriage to Paul after dropping out of college, the carefree early years of their marriage, the heartbreaking miscarriage, the doctor telling her she would never be able to have children, Paul's drinking, the arguments, more arguments…the lonely, quiet house she dreaded returning to after work, discovering Radio Rev's show… Hope, Karen…She slowed the car and parked a block from the Minor household.

Confident that no one was looking, she opened her car door and walked up the small hill. *They'll be home from the dance at any minute.* From her previous research, Lillian knew the long row of arborvitae that lined the driveway would shield her from view.

Please, God, give me a sign! she prayed. As carefully as she planned every aspect of her life, this was the one time Lillian had no concrete plan. She reasoned again, *This idea must have come from God, so I'm sure He will help me!*

She stood behind the emerald trees for several minutes before she heard an approaching car's engine. She held her breath, hoping it was the blue SUV.

No such luck. Loud music pumped through the car's speakers, and Lillian sunk further into the darkness. Through the branches she could see an old Jeep with its windows down, packed with what she guessed were high school boys. The rap music drowned out the sound of the crickets, and raucous voices spilled out of the windows. Cursing, obnoxious laughter, and a crumpled-up beer can flew out the window.

The guilt threatened to return. *What are you going to do, Lil? Kidnap them?*

To re-focus, she decided to use the strategy she always used to deal with uncomfortable feelings – pretend they don't exist. Over the years, she had pretended Paul didn't have a problem, pretended they didn't argue, pretended the doctor's words about the miscarriage didn't bother her. Pretended not to hurt.

Pretending used to work well. Lately, though, her strategy wasn't working. Too many negatives prevented her from denying the problems that were piling up around her like a heap of junk.

Is there a pattern here? Ever since I changed my life around, things have gotten more….

She refused to complete the sentence, even in her mind. *Of course life would be difficult,* she reasoned. *Life isn't always comfortable! Stop complaining and wait for your sign.* The mini-pep talked helped a little, and Lillian's breathing slowed as she waited.

Soon, she heard another car. This time, she held her breath for good reason: the blue SUV slowed to a stop on the driveway. Doors opened, and voices escaped from the car. Lillian heard Hope laugh, Karen's mom ask a question. Peering through the trees, she saw Karen dancing in the driveway.

If I didn't know better, I would think she was imitating James Tullo!

She could see Mrs. Minor unload groceries from the trunk as Hope jogged toward the house. *How am I supposed to get the girls with Hope's mother standing there?*

A soft noise startled her. *What was that? A voice? My own thoughts? The wind blowing through the trees?*

She couldn't be sure, but it sounded like something or someone said, "Not now... not now... not now."

Three times? Hmmm, the Bible does like the number three. Maybe it's not supposed to happen this way?

Then she felt the words – or heard them – again: "Not now."

Hope, Karen, and Mrs. Minor walked into the garage. With the door closed firmly behind them, Lillian finally felt her shoulders relax. She stepped out of the trees and onto the uneven sidewalk. An old streetlight illuminated her ill-fitting brown dress. Lillian looked down at the sleeves. It was as if she were looking at herself for the first time. She wrinkled her nose.

This dress is ugly! I think I hate it... yet my clothes seemed too flashy before. I *seemed too flashy before.*

For a moment, she allowed the thought to enter: *Would it be possible for God to accept me for who I really am – flashy and all?*

No answer. No more voices, either. All she heard were the crickets and the wind in the still spring night.

⋙◆⋘

She parked the car and walked up the short gravel path to her bungalow-style home. She carefully brushed past the overgrown shrubs that blocked the basement windows. *I need to figure out how to trim those shrubs and still shield the church. People wouldn't understand, and I'm not ready to explain myself. Not yet.*

With every step, one question swirled through her mind: *how am I going to get Hope before tomorrow?*

With a heavy heart, she walked through the foyer and down the stairs to the basement. She looked at the table in the middle of the rec room – ten brushes stood in a rack, neatly lined up like soldiers ready for battle. Paint, sketches, and a large sheet of glass covered the rest of the surface.

Lillian tried to relax. Finally, she smiled. Somehow, some way, she had a feeling that God would deliver the girls to her just in time. She sat down at the table to resume her work. Picking up the brush, she began.

CHAPTER 15

Secrets

HOPE

Friday 9:00 PM

The air enveloped us with a collective chill as we filed out of the gym to search for our rides. "Brrr! I'm freezing!" Karen shivered. I looked at her bare arms, wondering how she got by Mr. Vambles.

I grabbed Karen's wrist and led her through the lot. "Ow!" she protested, but I ignored her, knowing full well if I let go, Karen would wander off in an attempt to talk to Anthony one last time. She would try to get in a few last words and some final flirting, and then she would get swallowed up in the crowd while I waited in the SUV, answering my mother's well-meaning but awkward questions. Plus, it would take even longer to get home and put our plan into action.

"There she is!" I yelled over the loud voices that were used to shouting over deafening music. After a dance, it was always difficult to hear anything at a normal volume. My mom's blue car was wedged between two mini-vans. We carefully walked across the lot and hopped in the back seat.

"Hi, girls! How was it?" Mom looked over her shoulder at us and shivered. "Ooh, Karen, aren't you freezing? Here, take my sweatshirt.

You'll catch a cold going outside like that!" Before Karen could say yes or no, she tossed a balled-up sweatshirt into the backseat.

Karen unfolded the fleece hoodie and put it on without complaint. That was unusual, because Karen could be in the middle of Antarctica and still refuse a jacket. I guess she didn't want to upset my mom, knowing we'd be breaking other rules later that evening.

Mom was in her usual chatty mood. "How was it? Did you do dance with any booooys?"

We groaned. "Mom!" I protested. "Stop it!"

"What? Not ask Karen about the love of her life? What's his name— Arthur?" As an involved parent, Mom made it a point to know everything about my friends. Luckily, she didn't know about Eli, so Karen had to handle the grilling.

Unlike me, Karen didn't mind discussing boys with my mom. For her, it was just another excuse to mention Anthony. "It's Anthony, not Arthur, Mrs. Minor. And I did get to dance with him – at the end, of course." She smiled dreamily, and for once, I couldn't blame her. My own little mental video of Eli deliciously replayed itself over and over in my mind.

My mom was still interrogating Karen, and I thought, *Boy, Mom can be nosy.*

Karen launched in with the worst lead-in ever: "Y'know Miss Lil – "

I elbowed her in the ribs. Hard. She glared at me, but instead of flinching like I normally do when Karen's mad at me, I ran my index finger across my throat. My mom didn't need to think anything unusual was going on, and any talk of Miss Lillian was sure to sound strange!

Karen opened her mouth to respond, but her head lurched forward unusually fast. *What's going on?* I felt the seat belt tighten across my chest as my mother cursed under her breath.

I looked out the window. A black Jeep screeched past us and turned onto Vista View Drive. Two of the Killigan brothers were sitting in the front of the car, with a bunch of kids wedged in the backseat. Everyone in Hidden Hills knew that Mr. and Mrs. Killigan were a little crazy, and their son, Sean, was no exception. He waved his hand at us in a half-hearted apology.

My mom let several curses fly from her lips, followed by "…and who the hell do they think they are, pulling out into oncoming traffic?"

Karen and I laughed. "Mom! We heard that!"

My mom gripped the wheel, muttering, "My God, I can't believe that Sean Killigan! He almost got himself and all his passengers killed. Do his parents know what he's doing? And if they do, how can they live with themselves, knowing how that boy drives?"

Karen and I seized the opportunity to change the subject from Miss Lillian to Sean Killigan's driving habits. When that conversation faded, I changed subjects again. "So, Mom, did you happen to have a chance to make those cookies you promised us?" My mother's peanut butter cookies with Hershey's kisses in the middle had become a tradition whenever Karen slept over.

"Yes, I did. You're welcome," she replied before we could thank her.

Karen finally picked up on my plan to change the subject, and she proceeded to fill my mom in on every detail of the dance, including Mr. Tullo's break dancing. As we walked up the driveway to the garage door, Karen lay down on the asphalt and imitated the worm the best she could. It wasn't quite as good as Mr. Tullo, but I had to give her props for trying.

"Isn't Mr. Tullo the one who always dances?" Mom asked. Karen nodded as she ditched her dance and stood up again.

Mom scrunched up her nose – a sure sign she's trying to remember something – and asked, "Who's that other chaperone who always dances with him? Was it Miss…" She paused to think. I practically choked, knowing it would be just my luck that my mom would remember Miss Lillian's name.

"Miss…Briar, is it? Miss Briar? The new teacher?" Miss Briar, the math teacher, was probably in her late thirties, but in my mom's mind, anyone younger than forty was "new".

I stumbled over my words, trying to escape the questions. "Nah, I don't think it's Miss Briar. Just Mr. Tullo tonight. Anyway, where are those cookies?"

I rushed ahead, but as I approached the garage door, a small movement over my shoulder made me pause. *What's that?* I looked in the direction of the trees lining our fence. Out of the corner of my eye, I thought I saw a moving branch. *A bird, maybe?*

I looked again. Now nothing moved. But I could have sworn that something – or someone – was there. I could sense it. *Maybe it was an optical illusion.*

Mom, still on her cookie kick, laughed. "Calm down, dearest daughter. You'll get your beloved snack soon enough! I wish you were that excited to see me and your dad!"

I tried to relax, but I kept picturing the movement from the bushes that I was sure I hadn't imagined. *You're worrying too much,* I thought. *Always expecting the worst. As if there's a band of robbers descending on Hidden Hills!*

Karen caught up to me. "What's up with your mom? I'm beginning to think her memory is as good as mine! How did she remember that someone else dances with Tullo?"

"I dunno. Let's just go down to the basement. I can't take the stress of trying to dodge another mention of Miss Lillian!"

"I know," Karen agreed. "Does your mom have telepathy or something? She never mentions the lady, and now it's, like, all she can talk about!"

PAUL
Friday 9:00 PM

Mike slid the glass toward the man sitting by himself. "Where's your friend?" he asked. Paul answered, but the bartender had already turned away.

I'm just another nameless face to this guy, Paul thought. *Too many men like me at this place.* Too many unhappy lives drowned in a frothy combination of stale cigarette smoke, water marks, and beer.

Another man raised his hand in a gesture of thanks and threw a bill on the bar. *Mike profits from our misery.* Paul watched Mike pocket the tip and move on to the next customer, a graying man with a sad story just like everyone else at Sports-N-More.

Paul downed his drink in less than a minute, and then raised his hand for another round. Unfortunately, Mike was busy mixing a concoction for some old man who wouldn't stop talking. *What a pathetic sight,* Paul thought as he watched the gray-haired man tug on Mike's sleeve, asking him to listen to more of his sob story.

Paul looked around the bar and waved at the regulars. The Budweiser clock glowed nine o'clock. He checked his pocket again. He could feel the handkerchief, and he thought about how difficult it had been for him to purchase it on such short notice. *It's still there,* he mused. *And if this doesn't change her mind, I don't know what will!*

"Another one, Paul?"

"Yep, just one more. I've gotta date tonight."

Mike smiled. "Really? Who's the lucky lady?"

Paul smiled back. "That's my little secret. I can tell you one thing, though. She's gonna be so shocked when she sees me, she won't know what hit her!"

RADIO REV
Friday 9:15 PM

Home at last.

Glenn lay down on the sofa and flicked on the television, hoping the mindless distraction would allow him to unwind. He wanted to be well-rested. *Tomorrow's a big day.*

But his anxiety about the revival and the worry he had experienced most evenings prevented him from relaxing. He tried to push the fear away, but it was always there: the fear that the dream would return again tonight.

The dream was nothing new. Several years ago, he had the first one. It was always the same – Caroline, looking beautiful as ever, telling him they both made mistakes in high school, Glenn agreeing, and just as they were trying to figure out how they could make the relationship work, he would wake up.

The first time it happened, he couldn't concentrate for days. He would look into a crowd of people and every face looked like Caroline. When a call would come in at work, he could barely understand the words – her voice was all he heard. And when he finally forced himself to forget the dream, all of the real memories from high school and beyond flooded his consciousness…

When she left for college years before, Glenn didn't know what to do with his energy, so he channeled it into anything and everything – sports, church, family, community college. Anything to forget her. If he wasn't on the football field, Glenn could be found with his dad and the Sunday School program. He became a counselor for summer church camps, and when he returned from Camp Oni-Son in August, it was time for football training to begin. Relatives filled his idle hours as well – Sunday dinners and unannounced visits allowed him to forget Caroline.

Almost forget, that is. Though the heartbreak faded over the years, there were times a memory would resurface in the unlikeliest situation and bring him right back to the excruciating pain he fought so hard to prevent.

The time it happened on the football field was the worst. It was the big grudge match against the rival community college. Football cradled in his hands, he glanced at the time left on the clock: 2:21.

Pow! There it was. *2:21. Genesis, chapter two, verse twenty-one:* "And the Lord God caused a deep sleep to fall upon Adam, and he slept: and he took one of his ribs, and closed up the flesh instead thereof."

It was the Bible verse Caroline challenged in science class that day with Mr. Leeds.

He had stopped dead in his tracks and felt a warm dizziness pass through his body. It was a miracle he hadn't dropped the ball. If it weren't for the help of two opponents' defensemen barreling into him to end the play, he would have fallen over, embarrassing himself further.

Coach didn't let him live that one down. "What happened to you out there? You looked like a deer in the headlights, and I know that can't be true, 'cause it ain't huntin' season yet! Now git yer butt out there and git yer head screwed back on the right ways!" Glenn just nodded and ran back to the field, pushing the numbers – and Caroline – out of his mind.

A loud commercial brought Glenn back to the present. He gripped the remote tightly, wishing the memory could simply stop haunting him. Glenn surfed through the channels, pausing on channel fifty. The documentary featured Jim Jones, the cult leader who led dozens of people to their deaths by brainwashing them into committing mass suicide.

For some reason, he found Jones' life oddly fascinating, yet the more he watched, the more he felt his stomach tighten and his heart beat faster. Watching the mesmerized faces of the leader's followers, Glenn felt an unsettling familiarity.

He jumped up and turned the television off.

CHAPTER 16

Go Time

HOPE

Friday 9:15 PM

Ahh, silence. Karen and I reveled in the privacy of the basement, the room where we would spend the night. I turned to my friend and smiled. "So?"

"So what?"

"So…don't you want to hear about my dance with Eli?"

Karen smacked her forehead. "Omigod! I almost forgot. Tell me all about it!"

I reveled in the delicious details, trying to recreate the feelings from earlier in the evening. It was difficult, though, to retell everything Eli said (and did!) and not be a little red-faced. Some things were too private to share, even with a best friend.

Karen whispered, "Be careful, girlfriend. Older men are more experienced!"

"What do you mean?"

"What I mean is…" and she proceeded to fill me in on every story she had ever heard about pregnant teens.

I held up both hands. "Karen, stop! You know Eli. Do you really think he'd be like that?" I tried to sound convincing, but I was beginning to have my doubts. *He is two years older, after all…*

Karen must have sensed my panic. "Calm down. I'm sure you're right. We've known Eli for years. Anyway, Patrick would murder him if he tried anything too freaky!"

I nodded in agreement, reassured that Eli would be a true gentleman. *But what if he wasn't? What would it be like to have Eli try something "freaky"?* I forced myself to remain calm, calling to mind Karen's teens-gone-bad stories. *I'm a good girl, and Eli must know that. Plus, my brother really would kill him if he tried to take advantage of me!*

Karen glanced at her watch and rubbed her hands together nervously. "So, when's go time?"

"What do you mean?"

"I mean, when are we gonna sneak over to Miss Lillian's?"

"Oh. Right." Clearly, talk of Eli was over for the evening.

My stomach churned, and I knew it wasn't from the cookies. *Who did I think I was fooling with those bold statements?* Coming off of the adrenaline rush of dancing with Eli, it was easy to sound adventurous and rebellious. But now I wasn't so sure this plan was the best one.

I decided to be up front. "I don't know, Kar. Do you think it's really worth it to sneak out? I mean, we've got my mom's cookies, the pizza, and all these movies to enjoy…" I looked at my friend hopefully.

Karen sat quietly for a minute. Then two. *Wow,* I thought. *She must be really sick of getting grounded!* Normally, Karen was the fastest-thinking girl I knew. She could listen to the most complicated stories or directions – anything, really! – and somehow know the answer faster than immediately. It was nothing short of amazing. She began speaking slowly, picking up momentum as she continued.

"Here's what I think. One, I can't get this off my mind. My reporter's instinct tells me this is the story of a lifetime! I can almost feel in my bones that this story will really, truly – don't laugh! – be my big break into journalism. But, y'know, I'm not just thinking of myself. This will help Miss Lillian, too."

I arched an eyebrow. "How is this good for Miss Lillian?"

Karen babbled on. "Well, I know we might get in trouble and all, but I'm starting to think it's worth the risk. Look how upset she was tonight! I mean, she might have a serious breakdown or something, and if anything bad happened to her, and we could've done something to prevent it, well…" She paused dramatically. "I don't think I could live with the guilt." Karen lowered her eyes and then peeked up at me.

I mulled it over. Despite Karen's lame excuse for helping Miss Lillian, I had to admit it would be exciting, fun, and very rebellious – words people don't tend to associate with me or my Friday night plans. And I did want to "find my voice", didn't I? No one said change was easy.

It was time to do something out of the ordinary. I mean, I'm in high school now. Aren't these supposed to be "the best years of my life"?

Plus, I really did like Miss Lillian. At least, I liked the *old* Miss Lillian. *What if Karen's right? What if she goes off the deep end?* An image of Miss Lillian sobbing in the hallway stuck in my mind. I couldn't erase the memory.

Karen's right, I decided. *This can't wait 'til Monday. It may be too late by then!*

I took a deep breath. "Karen, you're right. Sometimes, it's important to do the right thing, even if we risk getting caught. Miss Lillian's crazy with a capital 'C', but she might need help. Plus, doesn't everyone always say it's important to help those in need?"

We worked out all of the details, scribbling notes in my journal. As we plotted, Karen suggested, "Let's get some more food first, 'cause if we get caught, we're not going to be eating for a long, long time!"

CHAPTER 17

Stained Glass

LILLIAN

Friday 9:30 PM

Lillian held the delicate glass up to the light. "It's beautiful," she breathed softly. After days of hard work, it was finally complete. She took in the full effect of the brilliant colors playing against each other on the faux stained glass window she had fashioned for the basement. The iridescent shades reminded her of something, but she couldn't put her finger on it.

Then she remembered. "My old clothes!" Her long, flowing skirts seemed to dance through the patterns and color combinations on the glass. *Hopefully, God will like the colors and not find them too fancy!* But she didn't really believe that anyone, including God, would have a problem with this window. Clearly, any window that was not broken like the one in her basement was an upgrade. And certainly, no one else in her neighborhood would have a window quite like this one!

She looked across the room at the other window she had finished painting the week before. Though proud of her initial attempt, she had learned from her mistakes on the first one, and the second window was clearly superior.

Now, when I listen to Radio Rev, I can feel like I'm in church. I can pretend I'm in a big, beautiful cathedral with the powerful Reverend holding court at his podium.

The stained glass was the only part of her basement that resembled anything church-like, but Lillian enjoyed referring to the area as her church. She did have a grand plan for the space, though: ditch the ratty sofa and replace it with wooden pews. Of course, she would need to learn woodworking first. Next would be the organ. As an accomplished pianist, she knew she had the musical ability to learn to play the organ, even with its difficult pedals and dual keyboards. Purchasing the instrument would be the most challenging part. With Paul out of the house, her paychecks barely covered the mortgage, much less a basement renovation. However, Lillian had always believed that perseverance would pay off. *Why else had I stayed with Paul for so long?*

As she continued to plan and think, she carefully walked the window up the stairs to the kitchen. Now that the paint was ready to dry, she wanted to give it the full twenty-four hours of sunlight the directions suggested before installing it in the basement. She laid several tea towels across the oak table to cushion the glass.

She looked out the kitchen window and tried to find the moon, but the clouds were too dense. *So dark tonight. With the fog, it would be impossible to see anything more than a foot away!* She felt her shoulders relax with the realization that Hope and Karen would not have been able to see her spying on them in the bushes through the thick fog.

She glanced at her watch. 9:15. *Guess I'd better start cleaning up for the night.* She felt a momentary pang of disappointment, but she pushed the feeling aside. *Looks like I'll be going to the revival alone.*

CHAPTER 18

Point of No Return

HOPE

Friday 9:30 PM

"Camera?"

"Check!"

"Voice recorder?"

"Check! Karen, why are we bringing all this stuff? Your cell phone will record and film anything you want."

Karen whispered back, "I know, but the props make it more official. Plus, you know how unreliable my phone is. What if it went dead and I missed the perfect shot? The perfect interview?"

I shot Karen a horrified look. "You're not planning on talking to Miss Lillian, are you?" That definitely wasn't part of the plan.

"Of course not! I'm just saying..." she trailed off.

"C'mon, Karen! We agreed to take a few pictures of the house, maybe catch a glimpse of that basement church from the backyard. That's it! Then we can go home and relax. You know, gossip, eat, and talk about Anthony some more." The prospect of talking about Anthony was lost on Karen. She was too busy shoving the equipment into her backpack.

"How did you get Miss Lillian's address, anyway?"

Karen grinned. "Don't worry about how I got it. I've got people, y'know…"

I knew better than to ask who her "people" were. For as much as I admired Karen's determination, her methods didn't always involve the most savory classmates at school. Getting the address most likely involved an exchange of cash with the group of students who dressed as if they were headed to a funeral and always traveled in packs like wolves. They weren't in any of my classes, but I noticed them whenever I walked to the public library. They stood near the doors, lingering with their scowls and cigarettes.

We walked upstairs and into the kitchen. For good measure, I tossed a bag of popcorn in the microwave. Mom was already lounging on the couch, and my dad was attacking a bag of potato chips. I recited my rehearsed lines: "Hey, Dad, can you get the movie cued up for us? Patrick's always got the thing hooked up to his stupid Xbox, and he'll kill me if I ruin one of his precious games."

My dad sighed and hoisted himself up with Herculean effort. "OK, let me take care of it. And then you two are set, right? Because the next time I sit down in this chair, I'm not getting up, so you'd better handle all your requests now!" He smiled at both of us.

"Sorry, Dad. I know you're tired, and I promise, the movie is all we need. We'll be quiet as church mice for the rest of the night!" As the words escaped my lips, I regretted my reference to church.

We followed him to the basement. Once he finished setting up the movie, we chorused, "Thanks, Dad!"

He laughed again and glanced at both of us. "No problem. You two are so inseparable, I feel like I really do have two daughters!" And with that, Dad retreated to the La-Z-Boy for the night.

Based on years of sleepovers, we knew that my parents were now officially done for the evening. Mom might slip down the stairs at 1:00 or 2:00 in the morning after waking up on the sofa, but even that was rare. So unless they decided to change their routine for the first time ever, we would be safe for the next three to four hours. *Plenty of time to make a quick trip to Axel Court.*

Once we made our way outside, we looked at each other. I spoke first, gushing with excitement and nervousness, "It's time, Karen! Let's go before I chicken out!"

LILLIAN
Friday 9:45 PM

She returned to the basement and said a quick prayer as she flicked the lights off.

"God, can you hear me? It's your Lil' Lady! Anyway, I guess going to the revival solo is better than not going at all. But Lord, I was really hoping to save a soul. I really thought that you meant for me to help Hope! Karen, too, I guess. If I was wrong, that's OK. As You always said, 'Thy will be done.' But…"

A muffled noise from the basement's utility room interrupted her prayer. Her eyes darted towards the open door of the small room she and Paul used for storage. A quick flash of light emanated from the doorway. Lillian jumped.

"Hello? Anyone there?" She tiptoed towards the door. "God, is that you?" When no one responded, rational thought took over. She reached for the baseball bat she had been carrying around the house ever since Paul left. Quietly, slowly, she padded in the direction of the doorway. Even though there was a window near the door, the foggy night sky did nothing to illuminate the small room.

Lillian gripped the bat tightly and moved forward into the darkness. With a shaking hand, she pushed on the wooden door, creating an opening wide enough for her to move through. The old door protested with a creak before allowing her to enter. She peered into the inky darkness.

When she saw the two figures, she forgot all about the bat and let out a blood-curdling scream. Panicked, she madly ran her hands over the wall, searching for the light switch. After what seemed like an eternity, she felt the switch and flicked the light on. Her eyes bulged with disbelief at the spectacle before her.

HOPE

Friday 9:45 PM

"Karen, this is insane!" I whispered. "We've officially crossed the line and entered misdemeanor territory! I can't believe you talked me into this!"

I looked around the cramped space. A broken window had provided the entry Karen was looking for. I couldn't believe it. We were standing in the middle of a storage room in Miss Lillian's basement!

When we had arrived at the house earlier that evening, we quickly learned that nothing newsworthy was happening on the outside. After unsuccessfully trying to peek into windows at the front of the house, we scurried into the back yard. A ribbon of light escaped through a single window. We crept toward the house and peeked inside. It was the kitchen, and from the looks of it, Miss Lillian kept a clean house. The only things on the countertops were a few tea towels. Otherwise, every surface was bare.

I had said, "Maybe she's making cookies, and she's going to cool them on the towels."

Karen had sniffed the air. "Nah, I don't smell anything. Those towels must be there for another reason."

Before we could speculate any further, we saw a door swing open. "Quick! Move away! There she is!" We ran around to the side of the house, panting more from excitement than exhaustion.

Karen jabbed me in the ribs. "Omigod, Hope, look! A passage to the basement..."

I looked at the side of the house. There it was. The broken window that clearly led to part of Miss Lillian's basement...and the basement church. *Was it really true?*

Karen pressed on. "Let's check it out! I've gotta see it for myself. If there's a church down there, I want to be the first reporter on the scene!" Karen looked like she was ready to drool from the excitement of being this close to a breaking story.

As we inched closer, we could see that the window had a small crack in the glass, and the handle was completely sheared off. I whispered, "It looks like someone cut the handle off!" A steel handle would never break off so cleanly. *What – or who – did this?*

Karen pulled out her cell phone to take a picture. She hit a button several times and frowned. "What'd I tell ya? My phone died – again! Of all times..."

She cast a wicked grin my way. "Good thing I brought this!" She pulled the Canon from her backpack and zoomed in. After a minute or two, she stamped her foot in the flower bed and whined, "I can't see inside the basement from here! The window must lead to a smaller room. That's why we can't see anything."

She considered the situation briefly and said, "Hmm...guess we're gonna have to go in!"

As the words sunk in, I had to stop myself from yelling at her. Instead, I whispered, "Go in? What are you, nuts? We're not breaking and entering!" Surely, Karen would realize how stupid this latest idea was!

I was wrong.

Karen's voice shook slightly, but I couldn't ignore the sense of resolve. "It's not breaking and entering. The window's already broken, so it's just entering."

"We can't do that! Remember our deal – look but don't touch? You agreed, I agreed, and trying to pry the window open and climb in would definitely be way more than looking!"

Karen dug in her heels – literally. With frustration, she forced her sneaker into the mulch bed, creating a small divot. "But Hope! We're so close to this … I can feel it! And Miss Lillian's upstairs, so she'll never know. We'll get in, get out, and be done with it. A couple quick snaps of the camera, and voila! We've got ourselves a news story. And I've got myself the start of a career!"

The gleam in her eyes bore into me, and I felt myself weaken, as usual. *Why does Karen always have this effect on me?* Now she was tugging my hand as she pulled me toward the window.

I had just finished reading Chapter Four before the dance, and the key point – "push yourself beyond your comfort zone" – was too coincidental for me to ignore. *Is this a sign? Would this be a good way to push myself beyond my comfort zone?*

The window popped open with surprising ease, and perhaps more shocking was how large the opening was. Within two minutes, Karen had shimmied through. She whispered, "It's easy, Hope! There are boxes stacked up like steps. Just crawl through, and you can get down in no time flat!" Her head disappeared as she lowered herself into the space.

I took one final look around and listened intently. All I could hear were the passing cars on the main road a block away. Otherwise, the night was foggy enough that I knew it would be difficult for anyone outside to see me. Trying not to think about how wrong this was, I crouched down in front of the window and quickly dropped my right leg into the darkness.

"What the …" I whispered. A hard object met my foot and prevented me from free-falling. *There's box number one,* I thought as I lowered my other leg onto the box and hoisted myself downward. Karen was right – getting my feet on the ground was as easy as walking down a short set of stairs.

Though the small space was dark, a faint light seeped in from the rest of the basement. As my eyes adjusted, I could see Karen's silhouette. Though I still didn't see anything newsworthy, she reached for the Canon again.

I suddenly had a horrible thought. "Karen, wait! Don't forget to turn of the fla…"

Before I could finish, a loud clicking sound broke the silence, and a bright flash of light radiated into the rest of the room. Karen recoiled in horror. "Oh, shit! I forgot about the…."

We froze when we heard the high-pitched voice. "Hello?" a familiar voice asked. "Anyone there?" The voice continued, "God, is that you?" Karen and I looked at each other and shrugged our shoulders. *God? What was going on?*

Miss Lillian stopped talking, but I didn't take that as a good sign. *Where did she go?* If the steps in this house were anything like ours, we would've heard the person on the creaky stairs. I sensed that she was still near the door to the tiny room we stood in, though I couldn't be sure. Karen was blocking my view of the rest of the basement, and I was still standing where I had entered from the window — in the back corner, between a pile of luggage and the stairway of boxes.

A soft rubbing sound caught my attention. I took a deep breath and tried to regulate my shallow breathing.

Another flash of light blinded me. Someone had switched on a light! Once my eyes began to focus, I realized the figure before us was none other than Miss Lillian, brandishing a large baseball bat in her hands!

I shrieked, "Please stop! It's us!" Instinctively, I squeezed my eyes shut and put my hands over my head, expecting to receive a crack on the skull at any moment.

The bat clattered to the ground, and I peeked. Miss Lillian's eyes bulged out of her head. The Louisville Slugger rolled across the floor, coming to rest next to the pile of boxes. I glanced at Karen, who still covered her head with her hands.

Oh, boy. It's going to be a long night.

CHAPTER 19

Look Who's Coming to Church

PAUL

Friday 10:00 PM

He closed the car door quietly. *No need to arouse suspicion.* With the thick fog, Paul knew the mist would shroud the car from view. He could follow through with the plan. *No one will ever know I was here.*

With a careful yet purposeful gait, any passerby would realize that this was a man on a mission, and nothing was going to deter him from it. As he approached the bungalow his footsteps slowed.

With a quick glance to be sure no one was watching, he slipped between the neighboring houses and stopped to catch his breath. The smell of beer and whiskey turned his stomach, but he ignored the feeling and approached the window.

He peered into the lower level of his former home. The lights were on. Paul took a step closer and reached for the place where the window handle should be. *Yep, still broken. Just the way I like it.*

Mentally, Paul reviewed his plan one last time: *(1) Sneak into the utility room, (2) Start asking questions, (3) Make her answer those questions… all of them. No matter what. Whether she likes it – or not.*

HOPE

Friday 10:00 PM

I couldn't believe that we were actually sitting in the basement church, talking to Miss Lillian. The whole evening had a surreal quality about it, and if I weren't completely awake, I would have thought I dreamed up the entire evening. I tried to focus on the woman's words, but my mind raced as I looked around. Fake stained glass filled one of the windows. Other than that, the room looked like most other basements, with wall-to-wall carpeting, some old chairs, and a table with scattered papers on top. Miss Lillian grabbed one of the papers and waved the page in our faces.

"… See, this is how I want the pews to look. Of course, there won't be too many rows. I don't think many people will be attending these services…"

I barely noticed the intricate designs she had drawn. Instead, I glanced in Karen's direction. She had the same deer-in-headlights look.

"So, girls, that's all there is. I like church. I don't go out much, and I decided to bring the church to my house! Probably not as exciting as you had hoped, Karen."

Karen just stared at Miss Lillian blankly. Miss Lillian took that as her cue to keep talking: "I wish I had a story for you to put on the news, for your sake, but I don't have one. My life is relatively boring and quiet, and I know enough to understand that boring lives don't play well on television."

Karen's shoulders slumped, defeated. Her dreams of instant fame and fortune floated out through that broken window the more Miss Lillian talked about her boring life.

"I'm glad you're not angry with us," Karen sighed.

Lillian giggled. "Don't be ridiculous! I could never be angry with you sweet girls!"

Karen raised her eyebrows. "Does that mean you won't have to tell our parents about this?"

Miss Lillian looked heavenward, as if the Lord himself were going to shout out the answer.

"Well, I just don't know. You snuck out of Hope's house, broke into someone else's home, and completely invaded my privacy. Even though I hold no grudge against your curiosity, it's obvious that if I keep quiet on this one, you girls will be getting away with something your parents would certainly not approve of."

My stomach tightened. Even though my parents weren't as strict as Karen's, my mom and dad would definitely be furious about this adventure. I wouldn't be surprised if my parents decided to cut off some of the freedoms they had granted me over the years, now that I wouldn't be deemed trustworthy. *And that punishment would be sure to include no dates!* I thought about Eli and our Saturday night plans.

Please don't turn us in, Lillian! Please!

I studied Miss Lillian's face. Her eyes closed briefly, and when they opened I could see a sparkle in them. *Is she going to cry?*

When she spoke, it was the voice of a different person. More confident. More resolved. "Girls, the more I think about this, the more I think we can make this a win-win situation."

I looked over at Karen, whose expression couldn't be mistaken for anything other than desperate hopefulness. *Right now Karen is living up to my name more than I am: I don't feel an ounce of hope about this 'win-win' situation. What could we possibly have that Miss Lillian wants?*

CHAPTER 20

Striking a Deal

LILLIAN

Friday 10:00 PM

After the girls finished explaining why they had broken into the house, Lillian closed her eyes in prayer.

Thank you, Lord, for bringing these girls to me. Now I know why you wanted me to wait. Letting them come to me was genius! She opened her eyes. The light of God had shone into her heart, she was sure. She chose her words carefully.

"The more I think about this, the more I think we can make this a win-win situation."

Hope looked at Karen, doubt etched in her features, but Karen was looking across the table with a face so desperate it was almost frightening.

"We'll do anything!" Karen pleaded. "Really! Anything so I don't get grounded – again."

Lillian spoke quickly, figuring the less time they had to think, the more likely they would be to agree to this somewhat crazy scheme.

"OK, here's the plan: you girls head on home, and we'll pretend this never happened. I only ask for one thing in return." She paused dramatically. "Meet me here tomorrow morning at 5:30 to accompany me to a special ... umm, presentation. Yes, that's right! A presentation."

Karen's face fell. "5:30? In the morning?" Lillian nodded. "We don't even get up that early on school days!"

Hope agreed. "I like the not telling our parents part, but what kind of presentation are you talking about? And how are we supposed to come back here without anyone getting suspicious?"

Lillian giggled, trying to stay calm. She was so close to getting what she wanted – what she needed. *This is almost too easy. You'd better explain religion better than the last time you spoke to Hope about the topic!*

She began, "Well, there's this radio station I like, WFAM. Are you two familiar with it?" Both girls shook their heads. "No? That's okay. Anyway, it's a family station with talk shows and songs. I happen to have three tickets to one of their events, and, wouldn't you know? It's tomorrow morning. Don't worry. It's all very family-friendly and inspiring. In fact, you could tell your parents this would count towards your community service hours at school."

Even though Lillian knew that going to a revival would probably not count towards the Roosevelt students' mandated hundred hours of community volunteerism, she would cross that bridge when she came to it ... after she got them to go. It was a community event, so that part wasn't a complete lie.

Karen voiced her concern. "I don't know, Miss Lillian. How are we supposed to explain that we suddenly want to wake up early from a sleepover to go to this presentation of yours?" Hope nodded at the surprisingly rational logic.

Hmm, this may not be as easy as I thought. Well, God shows mercy for His children, but He also admonishes them for wrongdoing. Maybe I need to do a little bit of both.

Lillian coughed, and she tried to make her voice sound stern. "I understand, girls. I'm throwing something at you without much time to think. That's fine. Seems to me we're back to where we started, then."

She paused and picked up a pencil. "I guess it's time to call your parents. Hope, what's your family's phone number?" She poised the pencil above a bright pink Post-it.

Karen grabbed Miss Lillian's hand. "No, no, no! I wasn't saying we wouldn't go, I was just, umm, y'know … asking some questions … that's what all good reporters do…"

Karen's voice trailed off, but Hope still looked petrified. Lillian sighed and smiled.

"Then it's settled! Now, let's get you girls home before anyone knows you went missing."

HOPE

Friday 10:15 PM

What is Karen doing? Is she actually saying we'll do this thing? I couldn't believe my ears. One moment, Karen was speaking with logic, and now she was talking nonsense. *Just because she doesn't want to get grounded—again!*

I felt torn. While I wanted to avoid trouble, another, tiny part of me felt a sudden surge of excitement. Here we were, on the edge of getting into major trouble, a situation I had never been in. *Is this how finding your voice feels? Or am I just discovering my insane side?*

Before I could speak, we heard a loud scratching noise. I glanced in the direction of the utility room, where the door moved slightly. A coldness ran through my body as I saw the brass doorknob twist and turn.

No one else seemed to notice. I wondered if my eyes were playing tricks on me, but what I witnessed next made me gasp. The utility room door opened, and someone tall, wearing a ski mask, stepped into the room.

Karen's icy fingers grabbed my hand and I squeezed her hand back to acknowledge the fear we both felt. He (or she?) began walking towards us, and what happened next defied all logic. Instead of freezing in terror like most people would in this kind of situation, Miss Lillian leaped out of her chair and ran in front of us. For a moment, I remembered reading something about the fight or flight response in animals. *Miss Lillian must be a fighter.* She stood between us and the intruder like a mother bear protecting her cubs.

Her words were fierce, but her voice shook. "Take anything you want! Do what you need to do! I don't have much, but take whatever you need. But, don't you *dare* think of doing anything to these precious girls!" The more she spoke, the more we could see her arms tremble – almost uncontrollably.

Don't cry, Hope. Not now! I repeated over and over in my mind, but the predictable tears ran down my cheeks. I sniffed angrily, still gripping Karen's hand, while I allowed my free hand to hastily mop up my face.

Without warning, Lillian released her grip on us. I turned to see her step back and squint. "Paul?" she asked.

Karen and I looked at one another. *Miss Lillian knows this person?*

The figure exhaled, as if he were completely worn out from a long journey. Miss Lillian walked over and tugged at the ski mask. The man raised his hand to his face in a half-hearted attempt to stop her, but once his face was visible, his body language screamed, "I surrender!" With slumped shoulders, the man sat on the ground and put his head on his knees while hugging his legs.

Lillian repeated, "Paul? What in God's name are you doing?"

The man she called Paul looked up and said, "I'm back, Lil! This is my house, too! Apparently, even my best laid plans turn out wrong."

He reached into his coat pocket and pulled out a metallic container. Before anyone could react, he unscrewed the lid, raised the flask to his mouth, and guzzled the liquid inside. After several gulps, Paul shook his head and made a gravelly *Ahhhhhk* sound, as if it burned his throat. He coughed. "That's better!" he said.

I thought back to the time I mistakenly took a sip from my father's glass at dinner. The liquor had burned my throat, and Dad was laughing so hard he almost choked as he watched my disgusted and shocked reaction. He laughed, "I'm happy to see that response. No need for me to worry that you're going to start drinking anytime soon!"

But that was years ago, when I was still predictable old Hope. *What would Dad think if he saw me now?* I looked at the man in the rumpled clothes who took a few more swigs of alcohol and glared at the three of us.

Lillian sat down next to Paul. "Oh, Paul, even now you can't resist? You have to do that in front of the girls?"

"Do what in front of the girls? Relax a little?" He didn't wait for a reply, and, grabbing an identical container from the other pocket, downed the drink from that one as well. He laughed. "Lord knows I could use some relaxing! Getting kicked out of your own home is slightly – what's the word for it? – oh, yeah…stressful!"

The look he gave Lillian made me shiver. The tense tone of his voice hinted that one wrong response from us could signal danger. Miss Lillian must have sensed it, too. She softened her voice and put her right arm over Paul's shoulders. "Paul, I'm just saying…"

Paul recoiled from her comforting arm as if she had slapped him. He mimicked her high-pitched voice, "And I'm just saying…" His words sounded muddled and foggy.

He started over, apparently losing and regaining his train of thought. "I'm just saying that it's high time I reclaim what's rightfully mine!" His voice rose, and my new favorite word from that week's vocabulary list – menacing – came to mind.

Paul stopped to look at us as if he were seeing us for the first time. "Who are these girls, anyway?" He turned to Lillian and almost shouted, "What, are ya' doin', bringin' yer work home witcha?" He laughed at his own joke.

Miss Lillian spoke slowly. "Yes and no, Paul. These two young ladies go to Roosevelt, but I was just inviting them to the WFAM Revival. Isn't that nice?" She was speaking in a sing-song tone, just like my old kindergarten teacher. I could almost picture Miss Lillian getting ready to pull out the mats for nap time.

The questions raced through my mind faster than I could answer them: *Did this man have major issues? Like, is he one of those deranged lunatics you hear about on the news? And what did Miss Lillian mean by a revival?*

Paul seemed to read my mind. "What revival? If I didn't know you any better, Lil, I'da thought you're talkin' 'bout one of those crazy tents with everyone shouting 'Amen'! And what's WSAN, anyway?" Paul reached into his pocket again.

Now Miss Lillian talked even faster. "Not W-S-A-N, Sweetie. W-F-A-N." She emphasized each letter as she spoke. "And no, it's not a place filled with crazy people, Paul. It's just a church service with music and a lovely pastor."

My head spun. *Church? Pastor? She's taking us to a religious revival? How is that a presentation?* Now I eyed them both with suspicion.

What else wasn't Miss Lillian telling us?

CHAPTER 21

Striking Out

PAUL

Friday 10:15 PM

The fool-proof plan proved that Paul was, once again, the fool. Lil wasn't having a date over as he had expected, but she was entertaining two girls. And taking them to a revival. *What's going on? How am I going to do this if they're around?*

The anxiety made Paul shake, and he didn't like feeling nervous. It was time to use the tried-and-true friend that always managed to mellow him out. He finished the first flask and quickly felt the need for more. Despite Lillian's protests, he continued drinking from the container until the familiar numbness filled his body. He had to be careful, though. Too many times before, he'd pass the happy point and venture into the land of anger and insults.

If only I had been able to keep it under control. She didn't mind the drinking before. It was only when I turned into Mean Paul – as she called me – that she had a problem with my idea of relaxation.

Paul had made this promise many times before, this agreement to stop Mean Paul from emerging. But, as the drinking got worse through the years, he had a habit of waking up the next day with a pounding headache and the guilty realization that Mean Paul had reared his ugly head yet again.

He couldn't make any sense of this revival she kept mentioning. *Was it really like those Southern-style services – organ music competing with loud "Amens"?* In all their years together, they had never once gone to a church service, and they rarely discussed religion.

Though Paul had been brought up Catholic, his church involvement dwindled over the years. By the time he met Lillian, he had removed himself from any type of organized religion: he was too busy worshipping the altar of money. The sacrifices required of him to make the sale and close the deal made Paul feel like the martyrs he had read about in the Bible. *But Lillian had never been brought up with church, so why this newfound interest in religion?*

"Who's Radio Rev?" Paul asked suddenly.

Miss Lillian visibly jumped. "How do you know about him?"

"I think I should be asking you the same question….how do you know Radio Rev? Who is this person? Some new guy you're dating?"

Lillian sputtered, "Dating? New guy? Paul, you've got this all wrong. Believe me, I've never even seen the man, much less dated him! I told you, I'm not looking to meet someone new. I'm just looking for the man I met years before. You. Before all of…this." She motioned to the empty flasks he had dropped onto the table.

The familiar stab of guilt burned through Paul's heart. Last year, he had mistaken similar chest pains for a heart attack. He remembered the look of fear that etched worry lines in Lillian's face as they had driven at breakneck speed to the ER. Once they had gotten to the hospital, the doctors had realized how drunk he was and deemed the pains were all in his head. Now he would give anything to see that look of loving concern on his wife's face.

Without the sympathy from Lillian, Paul transformed the hurt into rage. He thought of all the sacrifices he made, the memories standing side by side like pictures from a twisted Hall of Fame. *Where's the appreciation for the years I worked to move up the ladder at Unicorp? And did you forget about all those nights I held you as you sobbed, knowing we could never have a child? Or how about the poker nights I'd abandoned a year into the marriage because you wanted more "together time"? Did you forget about that, Lillian? Or, are you too high and mighty now, with your revivals and prayers, to care?*

He felt his face getting warm. The fury intensified, as it always did after the drinking. He reached into the back pocket of his faded jeans to make sure it was still there. It was.

Time to pull this out?

Nah, not yet.

HOPE

Friday 10:30 PM

This was getting stranger by the minute.

Karen's head pivoted back and forth as Lillian and Paul's conversation volleyed like a tennis match. I found myself watching the drama unfold with disbelief. *If I didn't know better, I would think we were on a reality TV show!*

I glanced around the basement warily, almost expecting to catch sight of a poorly-hidden camera. If it were a prank, then this would all make sense. We could have a good laugh, and Karen and I could go home.

Based on the turn of events with Paul, though, I was pretty sure this was real and not a made-for-TV production. Getting in trouble didn't sound half-bad, either, as long as it meant we could get away from the unpredictable man who kept calling himself Lillian's husband. Even though he hadn't said anything threatening, it didn't take a rocket scientist to know the guy was unstable.

What if we do or say something and he freaks out? How are we going to get out of here?

LILLIAN
Friday 10:30 PM

Stay calm. Remember, Lil, this is Paul. Your husband. These pep talks had become increasingly common, especially since Paul changed. *Or,* she considered, *am I the one who's changed?*

With her new religious life, she kept telling herself she was a new person. But sometimes the words didn't ring true, like when the nurse tells you the shot won't hurt, but you know that it will.

After Paul rejected her consolation hug, she knew trouble was brewing. Enough recent phone conversations had proven to her how quickly he could turn nasty, and she wasn't sure how bad it might get when – not if – Paul took a turn for the worse.

She softened for a moment. *Maybe I've been too hard on him all these years. Maybe I'm the one with the problems, not him. Maybe….*

Stop it, Lillian! The other voice was back, the one that tried to tell her how to behave, how to live the "right" way. *You need to save people. Focus on the girls, not Paul.*

Just as quickly, the old Lillian argued back, *Look where you are now, doubting yourself all the time. You've forced yourself to forgo the smallest pleasures of life, like wearing your long, flowing skirts and bright colors. They used to literally brighten your day! Is this new you who you really want to be?*

Lillian shook her head in an attempt to hurl the inner voices out of the room. It didn't work. The lost Lillian … the scared Lillian … the hurt Lillian … the Lillian looking for simple answers … the Lillian who knew easy answers didn't exist … new life … old life … all of these rose to the surface and collided.

She couldn't block the competing voices anymore. It was too diffi-cult, too tiring. Lillian gazed at the stained glass. *Is it possible that I am all of these people?*

The thought escaped almost as quickly as it passed through her mind because Paul reached into his pocket again. *More alcohol?* She breathed easily when an empty hand emerged from the Levi's.

PAUL

Friday 10:45 PM

He looked around the room again. He locked his eyes on a large piece of glass that had obviously been hand-painted with bright colors. A cross here, a lamb there, and several random robed figures danced across the glass. Despite himself, he admired the careful work and skilled painting. He was finding it difficult to stay angry while look-ing at the calming images as he surveyed the rest of the room: large pieces of wood against the wall, a pile of "how-to" woodworking manu-als, paintbrushes, small bottles of paint, and, finally, two petrified girls sitting across from him, shaking in their seats.

Their obvious fear reassured him. *Wow, I finally found people who shrink in my presence. They sense my power over them.*

"So, girls, how old are you?"

Both answered, "Fourteen." The terror in their voices was unmistak-able now. Paul chuckled at his newfound power position.

"Hmmm, fourteen. Nice age, huh? Still young and innocent. Not a care in the world, eh?" The two girls reached for the other's hand. They gripped each other tightly.

Paul forced a grin. "No need to worry, girls. If you do as I say, you'll have nothing to fear…" he allowed his voice to trail off for impact, kind of like in the movies when the criminal has the victims tied up and tries to relax them before he does whatever it is that he marched into that scene to do.

Am I the bad guy? The criminal?

Hmph. Guess so.

Lillian stood up. "Paul, I've told you before, do what you want to me or this house. Just don't do anything – and I mean anything! – to these girls."

Paul snarled ominously, "Don't worry. I'm not going to do – " He made air quotes with his fingers in an attempt to mock her, "anything."

But in his head, he thought, *It's time.*

He smiled and said, "Before I go, Lil, I just want to give you something…"

The handkerchief cushioned the object in his back pocket. He grasped it and fiddled with the white cotton cloth. *Damn knot!* He couldn't work it loose from the handkerchief. He had the thing tied too tight.

Time froze when he heard the cracking noise. He struggled to loosen the stubborn knot, but his body leaned heavily to the right. More than leaning, now – everything looked sideways, and his right cheek brushed against what felt like carpeting. His left temple throbbed, and searing pain behind his eyes blinded him momentarily.

Why am I on the ground? He looked up at the bright fluorescent lights. He squinted, only to see Lillian standing over him, holding a long object in her hands. Paul's thoughts jumbled, and speaking became nearly impossible. *What was happening?*

"Lil…" He couldn't be sure the words escaped his lips or if he was just thinking her name. A black cloud descended from the ceiling, pulling Paul and his thoughts into a vacuum of nothingness.

HOPE

Friday 10:45 PM

Everything in the room became dark.

My hands!

Instinctively, I had put my hands over my face to block out the scene before me. I moved a few fingers away from my eyes and peeked. All I could see was Miss Lillian, holding the wooden bat in her hands. She looked at the ground in front of her. I followed her stare to witness Paul lying at her feet, eyes closed, face strangely peaceful.

Some sort of wrinkled cloth lay next to him. It twisted carelessly around a shiny black box. I knew the rumpled white material hadn't been there earlier.

A faraway-sounding noise filled my ears. The sound got louder, and I looked over to see Karen, sobbing uncontrollably. As tears dripped from her face, she shrieked at Miss Lillian. "You've killed him! And we were witnesses and didn't stop it! We're accomplices…"

My head spun as Karen's words sunk in. *Accomplices in a crime? Murder? Oh, shit.*

Karen babbled, "Well, in your defense, it did look like he pulled out a gun! I guess you were just trying to protect us. That's self-defense right? Isn't that what a jury would call it?" Karen continued asking questions without giving anyone time to answer. Miss Lillian stood frozen in place, still holding the bat, still staring at Paul.

I walked over to her. "Miss Lillian?"

Looking in the woman's saucer-like eyes, I could tell she was in shock. So, I did what I'd seen in the movies. I grabbed her by the shoulders and gave her a good shake. Well, as much of a shake a girl can give when someone's scaring the crap out of her!

Miss Lillian blinked and focused her gaze on me. "What did I just do?"

I tried to remember what had happened before I put my hands over my eyes. Paul had been reaching behind his back for something. *Another drink, probably.* When his hands reappeared, a balled-up piece of white material peeked out from his fingers. If I hadn't known better, I would have thought it was a gun. Isn't that what everyone in a movie whips out when cornered? *But this is real life, not a movie,* I reminded myself.

Then Karen's words slid into my mind. She was always saying, "Bad things can happen anywhere. Even right under our noses! And that's when I'll find the real news story!"

Maybe Karen was right. Maybe this nightmare was taking an evil turn, and Paul was going to shoot us all. *I don't want to die now. I'm too young!* We wouldn't live to tell the truth, either. And all because of what? Karen's crazy dreams of stardom? My need to prove that I could be rebellious?

Everything else seemed so small. Grades? School dances? Guys? Gossip? *Those were my worries?* I took in the real-life crime scene that surrounded me and replayed the last several minutes over in my mind: Paul had said something, and without warning, Miss Lillian snapped into action. With one sweeping motion, she had bent over, picked up the bat, and took a swing that would make my sports-obsessed brother do a double-take.

Luckily for Paul, she appeared to have missed his face, but the tip of the bat made contact with his temple. Blood appeared instantly from the swiping force. Paul withered and fell like a brittle tree, blown over by the wind.

His eyes closed, and whatever he held in his hand dropped to the floor. Some of the handkerchief knot had loosened, and I could see its contents more clearly. Elegant gold-stamped letters covered the lid of a dark box. *Do you store a gun in a box like that?*

I looked around the room again, focusing on the present. I forced the memory of Lillian and the bat to the back of my mind.

Lillian's quavering voice filled the room. "What did I do?"

"I think you clocked him pretty good, Miss Lillian, that's what," Karen said with horror and fascination. And then, the question that only Karen had the guts to ask: "Is he…you know…?" Karen began. I knew what she was thinking. What all of us wondered. *Is he really dead?*

I stared at the still figure, willing the body to give us a hint of life – a rising chest, fluttering eyelids – anything! But Paul lay on the cold floor, motionless.

A loud chirping noise punctuated the tense silence, and the three of us turned to see a cricket. The bright sound contrasted sharply with the chilling scene before us. The insect crawled toward the small red stain near Paul's head.

I gulped. My dad, a volunteer EMT, once gave me a lesson in life-saving. He showed me how to locate a pulse with a doll named Resucianne. At the time, rescuing the fake doll was fun, but the prospect of using those skills now horrified me.

I remembered his words from that day. "You have to practice these skills until they are automatic. That way, in a true emergency, it's natural. A habit. You won't think twice about it, and you'll remain calm – maintain composure. Nothing is worse in an emergency than panicking." I looked over at Karen, who was failing Emergency 101. She sat in the chair, hyperventilating.

It would be up to me to help. Ignoring the blood on the floor and the pounding in my brain, I willed myself to stand. My legs felt heavy and tingly, as if they hadn't been used for years.

I shuffled over to Paul, and before I could chicken out, I leaned over to put my fingers on his neck just as my dad had demonstrated. I applied slight pressure to feel the pulse that I prayed was there.

Several seconds passed, and I couldn't feel a thing. Some of the blood from his head stained my fingers, and I tried to forget everything I had ever learned about AIDS. My hand was shaking so hard, I wasn't going to notice anything, even if he had a pulse. I took a deep breath and exhaled hard, forcing my hands to steady themselves.

For the second time, I pressed my fingers into Paul's fleshy neck. Stubble scratched my fingers, and then, ever-so-slightly, I detected a tiny pitter-patter. I crossed two fingers on my free hand, hoping the feeling was accurate. After a few more seconds, I was convinced it wasn't my imagination. I stood up and smiled.

"He's alive! I can feel a pulse, but it's a little thready." I remembered my dad using that term – thready – with a patient whose pacemaker was failing. Both Karen and Lillian stared, waiting for more. "Good news, though – he's definitely alive!"

Karen jumped up. "We've gotta call 911! Miss Lillian, where's the phone?"

Mute, Miss Lillian pointed to a wooden desk with neat stacks of paper piled on top. An open Bible lay next to the phone. Karen ran to the desk and snatched the receiver, knocking the heavy book onto the floor. Miss Lillian gasped, but Karen ignored her as she punched three numbers and stammered, "Hello? Hi, we have an emergency. My name? Oh, uhh…I don't live here, but there's a man at this house with a head injury!"

Pause. "Did I do it? Who do you think I am?"

Another pause. "Oh, you have to say that to everyone? No, of course I didn't do it! Why would I be calling you if I did — "

Karen held the phone away from her head and gave it the finger. She whispered, "How rude!" Then she pulled the receiver back to her ear. "Uh, huh…yes, that's right. Okay, thanks!" She hung up.

"Well?" Miss Lillian and I chorused.

Karen turned to face us. The smug look made it clear that she was excited to have information we didn't.

"The 911 operator, though a little *rude,* said she will be dispatching an ambulance as quickly as possible."

"Karen, that's great news, but weren't you supposed to stay on the line?"

Her eyes opened wide, but not because of my words. She slapped her thigh and spun to face us. "Wait! Now what do we do? When the ambulance gets here, they're gonna figure out that we don't belong here, and then they're gonna call our families, and then…"

Tears pooled in Karen's eyes. Her face turned red with mounting anxiety. She was right. We were busted for sure. I pictured Eli texting me, but I wouldn't be able to answer. It would be difficult to use my phone after my parents smashed it into a million pieces. My dad, in various stages of anger over the years, had threatened take my phone and do unmentionable things to it. He never did, though. *If we get caught, tonight may be the night he'll follow through with those threats.*

"Unless…" Miss Lillian interrupted.

"Unless?" we demanded.

"Unless I hide you."

CHAPTER 22

Desperate Times

LILLIAN

Friday 10:50 PM

Lillian, what are you doing? Are you really going to try to hide these girls? You'll be guilty of a crime!

She forced the thoughts away and allowed the "New Lillian" to resurface. *Lil, Lil, Lil. Remember what you've learned? Sometimes God works in mysterious ways. This is one of those times. Hide the girls, get them to the revival, and save them – in more ways than one!* Both girls looked at Lillian with dread. Clearly, they were afraid of her now, and Lillian didn't like that. *Time to calm them down.*

"Girls, I'm not going to do anything to you! Seriously, I'm not like him," she said, motioning to the heap on the ground that was Paul. "I truly don't want you to get in trouble, and I meant it when I said I wanted you to accompany me to the revival. If you two get caught now, there's no way you'll be able to go, and I'll have to go alone." She tried to make her face look like a sad puppy dog, hoping the girls would feel sorry for her.

Either the face worked, or Karen's paranoia about getting in trouble took over. She sighed, "Miss Lillian has a point. Look at it this way: we've gone this far. Why not go all the way?"

Lillian turned to Hope, whose face did not match Karen's optimistic one. "I dunno, Kar...umm...let me think..." Her voice trailed off.

Lillian pounced on their uncertainty. "Girls, think about it...first, you snuck out of your parents' house, without their permission, I assume." Both girls nodded in agreement.

"Then, you stumbled upon some circumstances that were probably more than you bargained for, right?" They nodded again, imaginary question marks stamped on their faces.

"I don't want to put you in a more awkward situation than you are already in, but let me explain. This is my husband, Paul. It probably comes as no surprise to you, but he has a drinking problem. I'm trying to help him with that, but he hasn't been very cooperative."

Lillian tried to smile, but she knew she was forcing it and gave up trying. "Anyway, he's incredibly angry with me right now because I won't let him come back to the house until he's gotten some help. I'm sure you know how dangerous alcoholism is, and I hope you can understand that I can't bear to see him slowly kill himself."

Karen interrupted. "But you almost killed him yourself! You swung at him like Ryan Howard!" I almost laughed at my baseball-aversive friend's reference to the Phillies batter.

"Oh, that." Lillian waved her hand dismissively. "I just thought he was going to hurt you two. Believe me when I tell you I would never forgive myself if something happened to either one of you on my watch!"

Karen let the words sink in and allowed Lillian to continue. Meanwhile, Hope's face was devoid of emotion. Lillian had no idea what they would do or say next, so she lumbered on. "Here's what I think. I'm proposing another win-win situation. If you girls lay low for a few minutes, we can get Paul to the hospital, I'll do all the talking to the EMT's, and – "

Now it was Hope's turn to interrupt. Her face had a white pallor to it. "Did you just say EMTs?"

Karen snapped her head in Hope's direction. "Oh, noooo!" Karen moaned. Lillian was thoroughly perplexed at their reaction, and looked to Karen for an explanation. She clarified, "Hope's dad is an EMT, and he's on call tonight! That means he's going to be here any minute!"

HOPE
Friday 10:50 PM

I could picture it now: Mom and Dad, asleep on the sofa with Comedy Central commercials blaring in the background, glad the work week was over. Mom would be curled up on the far end of the sofa. Dad would be hogging the remainder of the couch, head on the arm-rest. The cell phone would ring, and Dad would sit up suddenly with a slightly disoriented look while he took the call. Then he'd hang up and say something to my mom like, "This one is close by, hon. Probably be gone less than two hours."

My mom would grunt, "Okay," but have no idea what he said because she would be half-asleep herself. Hopefully, he wouldn't notice the window that had been pried open. But it was only a matter of time before he would descend to the basement and spot his only daughter and her best friend sitting in the middle of a possible crime scene.

Karen is right. Coming clean at the moment would not be worth it. Not only would we be busted for sneaking out, but I could wave goodbye to my date with Eli. Knowing how seriously Dad takes the EMT thing, I might be in danger of never leaving the house again. A nightmarish image haunted me of sitting in my bedroom for the next four years with no friends or dates. At the moment, finding my "voice" seemed like the dumbest idea ever. It was time to shift into survival mode.

"Karen? Miss Lillian?" They both stared at me. I squeezed Karen's hand one last time before releasing it. "I think we should hide. This is getting worse by the minute, and you have no idea how important being an EMT is to my dad. None of us will want to deal with his anger if he finds us here. Miss Lillian, your husband is in the best hands. If anyone can save him, it's my father. When it comes to emergencies, he's the best!"

The pride I felt for Dad mixed with incredible guilt. *How could he be so noble and have a daughter who's screwing up so royally?*

I turned to Karen. "Miss Lillian's right. If the worst we do is tell a little white lie to make her happy and give her some company at this revival – or whatever it is – then no one is the wiser. We didn't do anything *that* bad, so why should we get punished into the next millennium?" For a moment, I almost believed my own speech. "Let's sneak out of here and somehow come back again in the morning. What time is the revival?"

Miss Lillian beamed. "Six A.M.! And it's a sunrise service. Doesn't that sound beautiful?"

Nothing sounded beautiful at this point. I ignored her question and sighed, "What do you need us to do?"

"Don't you girls worry about a thing! Be back here at 5:30. I'll drive. It'll only last a few hours. You should be home by eight-thirty...nine o'clock, tops."

I mentally calculated. Three and a half hours of being gone? What were we going to tell our parents? *Oh, well, we'll have the whole night – or what's left of it – to figure that out.*

I did a few mental calculations. *In twelve hours, all of this will be over. Everything will return to normal. No more sneaking out, and no more lies!*

If this is what being rebellious means, then count me out! I'll need to find my voice in other ways.

LILLIAN
Friday 10:55 PM

Is it really true? she thought triumphantly. *Did I really convince them to go?*

She began her mental preparations out loud. "Girls, I think the best way to do this is for you leave now, and then figure out a way to get back here in the morning. The last thing we need is for people to be snooping around here looking for you."

Both girls nodded, relief evident on their faces. Doubt quickly replaced Lillian's joy, however. *Would they really follow through? Will they come back in the morning?* She needed to ensure their return. *Some memorable parting words couldn't hurt.*

She said, "You do understand our agreement, right?"

"Yes," Hope said mildly. "But, what if we can't figure out a way to get back here?"

Lillian stared hard at the girls. "Well, you figured out a way to get here tonight. I'm sure you'll think of something."

"But if we can't…" Karen echoed.

"Then I guess…" Lillian paused for dramatic effect. "I'll have to call your parents and tell them what happened here this evening." She stopped to let the words sink in. Karen and Hope looked at the ground. *Probably feeling guilty because they were thinking they could get out of our deal.*

Always quick to answer, Karen piped up. "Don't worry – we'll figure something out. Right, Hope?"

Both girls laughed, but Lillian could tell it was forced. As much as she wanted to remain stern, she felt herself weaken. The girls were uncomfortable with her. *Don't they like me?*

"C'mon, girls! Why the long faces? It's not like I'm telling you to report to detention in the morning. You're really helping me out. You know, keeping me company and all. How often do you get to make an old lady feel good?" She smiled, and the girls' shoulders relaxed.

This time, Hope spoke. "You're not that old, Miss Lillian!"

"Yeah, but compared to you two, I must seem ancient!" Though Lillian knew she was far from old, she couldn't ignore the deepening laugh lines she noticed when she looked in the mirror. "Alright, then, let's get you two home and..."

At first, the noise sounded like a car alarm, but as it got louder, there was no mistaking the siren's scream. She froze with the realization that the siren was headed toward her house – and the girls!

And what about Paul? She looked at the lifeless heap on the floor. *Paul's still unconscious. Then again, his normal state of mind has been unconscious lately, so this is hardly new,* she joked uneasily with herself.

Without wasting another moment, Lillian barked out orders. "Go! Get in the utility room! Close the door behind you and leave the same way you came in. By the time the paramedics take care of Paul, you two will be long gone."

Hope and Karen almost flew into the room. They slammed the door behind them with a bang. Lillian jumped at the sound and said a silent prayer that they would escape in time.

After surveying the room, she decided to cover the stained glass window (*No need for extra questions. The police would already have enough questions of their own!*). She grabbed a fleece blanket from the couch and hastily covered the glass, tucking the loose ends of the blanket under each corner. She looked at the lumpy blanket. "Hmmm," she muttered, "That looks even stranger." She picked up the glass, whisked the closet door open, and almost dropped everything when she saw that Hope and Karen were still standing there.

"Why are you still here?" she hissed. "Go on, now! They're going to be here at any —" Her sentence was interrupted by a loud banging noise overhead.

Hope cried, "It's too late! When we tried to crawl out the window, the police were walking around your property!" Tears flowed freely down her cheeks. "Now what do we do?"

"Oh, dear!" She made a swift decision. "I guess you'll have to stay in here! Just don't make any noise." She eyed Karen sternly. "And no flash cameras!"

Karen's lips curved into a wry smile. "Don't worry. I've learned my lesson!"

The knocking noise rumbled through the house for a second time. "Keep quiet!" Lillian cautioned. She carefully laid the window-wrapped blanket on top of two boxes. "Coming!" she shouted loudly as she skipped up the stairs, two at a time.

A tall, muscular man in a dark uniform stood in the doorway. He looked at her briefly and looked past her down the dark hallway. The officer coughed, "Good evening. We received a 911 call from this address. Do you have an emergency?" He looked at her evenly, as if he were prepared to separate fact from fiction in anything she was about to say.

Lillian measured each word of her response carefully. "Why, yes, Officer, I do have an emergency. It's my, uhh, husband. Paul. Well, he's my husband, but he's not living here right now. But he is here right now. In the house, I mean. But not permanently. I mean…" Her voice trailed off when she noticed the officer's confused expression.

He responded with a noncommittal, "Hmmm." And then a half-question, half-observation: "Ma'am, you appear to be a little bit… distraught?"

Lillian's tense shoulders deflated with relief. "Yes, Sir, I am quite distraught! Who expects a husband to pass out like that?"

"So, he just fell over? Passed out, you say?" The eyebrows were raised again.

Lillian stammered, "Well, not exactly. See, Paul is having some drinking problems, and he has been very angry with me. Angry about everything, really –"

The officer cut her off. "Okay, ma'am, we can get into the details later. The ambulance should be here any minute to get him to a hospital. Where is he?"

"Right down here, Sir. In the basement." She walked slowly to the door. *I hope that the extra time we spent talking gave Hope and Karen a window of opportunity to escape.* She paused again. *Window of opportunity? No pun intended,* she thought dryly.

She glanced at the shiny silver badge on his jacket pocket. Officer Trevor Conlan. He followed closely behind her, and she could hear him speaking into his walkie-talkie: "We've got a 557 at 232 Axel Court. Male, named Paul Amadon, age —" He stopped. "Ma'am, how old is your husband?"

"He's forty-nine and a half. Almost over the hill as of July 23!" She stopped herself from talking. She knew her tone sounded way too lighthearted for a wife whose husband was passed out on the floor.

Why am *I so nonchalant?* she wondered.

Officer Trevor finished reporting the pertinent information and walked down the steps. They both surveyed the room: neat-as-a-pin, except for the heap of humanity on the floor.

"Passed out, you say?" Lillian said nothing as the officer looked at Paul and the small puddle of blood next to his head. He knelt down and put two fingers on Paul's neck. He exhaled with relief. "Slow pulse, but that could be normal for him. Is he an athlete?"

Lillian nodded. "He was. All-American football player at Gettysbury College. Still played two-hand touch with the guys from the office on Sundays, ran daily until about a year ago when he started with the…"

she stopped, remembering how the drinking, which always seemed good-natured before, had taken a turn for the worse.

It was those hour-long football games that turned into endless hours at Sports-N-More. Instead of leaving the bar when his friends did, Paul would close down the establishment along with the bartender. He would screech into the driveway, car parked askew, reeking of cigarette smoke and alcohol.

She winced at the repeated memories of a door swinging open, the figure staggering toward her, slurring her name. That's when the insults would begin. His face would turn bright red, and the loosely contained anger would surge forth like a tsunami. "Dammit, Lillian! Where are you when I need ya … an' wha's wrong with this house? I juz lef' it a few hours ago, an' now lookit! Looks like hell, that's wha…" And on and on. Sometimes he would rant for hours, and the worse he got, the more his highly-trained speech lessons would fail him.

Paul was a born-and-bred Southern boy, but when he attended college with the Yanks, as he called them, he believed he sounded too "folksy" with his southern drawl. After graduation, it only got worse. As a member of the high-powered sales team at Unicorp, Paul felt pressured to fit in more than ever. *How will anyone take me seriously if I sound like Andy of Mayberry?* he said to her on more than one occasion.

Now, years later, very few people would guess that Paul was a small-town boy from Mississippi. In fact, his grammar was so precise, his enunciation so perfect, that people sometimes mistook him for an erudite college professor. Of course, the more he drank, the less he could control his speech patterns, temper, or behavior. More and more, Lillian became the victim of the latent accent, mixed with venom and whiskey.

Some EMTs entered the room, and everyone began asking questions:

Why is his head bleeding?

What's the story with the baseball bat?

Ma'am, we really need you to tell us what happened.

Try as she might, she couldn't bring herself to respond. Instead, she stared at Paul, and she tried to feel her pain. Tried to feel sad. But instead, she felt nothing at all – his pain had left her numb and hitting him elicited no remorse. Knowing he may be seriously hurt didn't bother her like it should, either.

I must be a monster.

She stood limply as the EMTs loaded Paul onto the gurney and hauled him up the stairs and into the ambulance. Realizing she should be following them, she jerked to attention and walked up the stairs, thinking, *I'm hurt. And now I've hurt Paul.*

Officer Trevor was talking again: "Believe me, this isn't the first domestic dispute in this town that ended with violence. You seem like a nice lady, so I apologize for having to do this, but I really need you to come down to the station to answer a few questions…"

In a fog, she allowed the officer to lead her out the door of the bungalow. She felt as if she were floating from the porch to the back of the officer's sedan.

Looking around the back seat of the police cruiser, she saw nothing. White light blinded her, and all she could see was Paul's face. Eventually, the image vanished and the light shined so brightly that nothing else could come into focus. *Am I imagining this?* The words of the police officer faded, and she closed her eyes. She began to whistle, ever-so-softly. Somewhere in the distance, the officer's voice noted, "Isn't that *Amazing Grace?*"

Mindlessly, she nodded and continued the mesmerizing whistling. Soon, the only voice she could hear was that of Radio Rev. Calling her to fulfill her duty…calling…calling…

HOPE

Friday 10:55 PM

On our first attempt to exit the house, I had seen a huge, uniformed police officer turning the corner to enter the backyard. Luckily, he was looking the other way, and it gave me the extra seconds I needed to retreat into the safety of the basement.

Miss Lillian had returned to the basement, and even though she told us to leave, that officer wasn't leaving, either. He was poking around the shed, looking behind bushes. I knew it was only a matter of time before he noticed the footprints in the flower beds, the broken window leading to us, or both.

"Quick, Karen. Get behind that!" I motioned towards the hot water heater, a huge barrel situated in the middle of the room. If we huddled at just the right spot, we wouldn't be visible from the doorway or the exterior window. That's where we were sitting when we heard Miss Lillian and the officer walk slowly down the stairs.

"He's alive," I heard him say. A smile spread across Karen's face. Pride filled my heart, knowing I made the same diagnosis about Paul minutes before.

A loud thump above our heads made us jump. More people! What sounded like a herd of elephants got louder as they entered the basement. A familiar voice rose from the noise. *Dad!*

"Where is he?" Dad asked.

"Here," Miss Lillian's voice replied.

After a moment of silence, my dad's list of questions began: How did this happen? What time? How did Paul enter the house? What was the bat used for? How long has he been unconscious? Miss Lillian remained silent, despite their encouragement to provide them with vital information. She finally answered one question: "Who called 911?" I held my breath.

"Uhh, I did," Miss Lillian stated flatly. *Oh no, I thought, Dad will see through that lie in an instant.* He was so good at uncovering my brother's lies (or as Patrick called it, "stretching the truth"), that he could spot a made-up story from a mile away. Especially if the person paused first and said, "Uhh." That was the perfect clue that the truth and what the person said were two different things.

Apparently, Dad didn't seem to suspect Miss Lillian was lying, because he said, "Well, I'm glad we got here when we did. Even though his vitals look fine, it's impossible to know if the trauma to his head caused any internal swelling or bleeding. Only a CAT scan will tell, so the sooner we get him to Centennial, the better."

As the voices grew faint and the EMT's carried Paul up the stairs, the weight of the situation sunk in. We had just witnessed what could be an attempted murder, and even though Paul looked alright, he might have injuries we couldn't see from the outside.

All because she was trying to protect us. The stab of guilt returned and got worse knowing that Paul didn't have a gun. That little black box with the gold letters wasn't going to hurt us, and I was pretty sure Paul didn't intend to scare us, either. *For Miss Lillian to react so harshly... well, either she had a reason to fear him, or else she felt more protective of us than we knew!*

There were more sounds upstairs. I froze again and listened. "Ma'am, I'm going to have to ask you to come down to the station to answer some questions." There was a serious tone to the loud voice that made me worry for Miss Lillian's sake.

"What do you mean?" She sounded truly puzzled.

"Ma'am, you just told the EMT's that you hit your husband over the head with a baseball bat for no apparent reason. Now, I know you mentioned drinking and I have no idea what prompted you to take a swing at him. Believe me, it's not the first domestic dispute in this town that ended with violence. You seem like a nice lady, so I apologize for having to do this, but…"

I couldn't hear the rest, because the front door slammed shut. We could hear creaking footsteps above our heads from Miss Lillian's front porch. *Now what?*

This has to be a bad dream, I told myself. After blinking a few times and pinching myself, I faced the facts: I wasn't back at home waking from a nightmare, snuggled under down comforters on the pull-out sofa, Karen snoring next to me. No, this was real.

Did they arrest her? Would she be under oath? To tell the whole truth, and nothing but the truth? Would she need to tell the police about us? All these questions muddied the waters of my mind. One thing was clear, though: the house was finally empty.

"Whew! That was close," I breathed. "Let's go!"

I scrambled toward the window, but Karen pulled on the bottom of my sweater.

"Not so fast, Hope. Do you realize what this means?"

"That we're going to get in trouble tonight?"

"No... although you might be right about that. I mean, we're in this house. Alone. It's time to find what we really came for. This story is too juicy to ignore. If we're going to get in trouble, we may as well have a story to go along with the punishment!"

I couldn't believe it. Despite this fantastic turn of events, all she could think about was her crazy dream of being a star! I had to admit, though, that I was as curious as Karen. Plus, I had a feeling if our parents found out – and that probability was increasing by the minute – then we may as well make this adventure last a little bit longer.

It was strange: one minute I was hoping this night would be as far behind me as a bad dream, and the next minute, I found myself electrified and energized. This experience was a challenge to who I thought I was – Hope, the good girl. Hope, the conscientious student. Hope, the role model.

Even though I had gotten used to those labels over the years, it was a lot to live up to, especially knowing Patrick let my parents down so many times before. He was a fun brother, but words like careful and dependable weren't used to describe him.

The pressure was squarely on my shoulders to be the responsible child for the foreseeable future – unless, of course, my parents had another baby. But from years of eavesdropping, I was pretty sure that babies were not part of my parents' plan. That meant they would look to me forever to represent our family positively.

Teachers were always saying things to my mom like, "That Hope! She's nothing like her brother! What a joy to teach!" And even though it felt good in the moment, there were so many days I grew tired of it. Tired of the pressure. Tired of trying to be what everyone wanted me to be.

This is the time, a little voice inside my head whispered. *Time to do something unbelievable and out of character... something fun! And here it is – the opportunity to have the adventure of a lifetime. What are you waiting for? Another chapter in that book to give you permission?*

I made up my mind. "Karen?" She looked at me and waited patiently – for once. "I know I've said this before, but let's do it – before I chicken out – again!"

CHAPTER 23

Rock Bottom

PAUL

Friday 11:10 PM

Voices. *Lillian? No, it was a man's voice. What man? That Rev guy?* He listened closely.

"The lady said it was in self-defense, that she thought the old man was pulling a gun out of his back pocket, and that's why she wacked him."

Old man? Who are they calling an old man?

A different voice. Still male, but this one sounded like he had a head cold. "I'll tell ya, if I had a dollar for every time we've picked someone up for domestic violence in this town, I'd be rich!"

As the two joked about how deceptively violent their town was, Paul tried to lift his head. It felt like bricks had been inserted into his brain to anchor it; the more he raised his head, the more he felt something sharp dig into his neck.

"Whoa there, Buddy! Don't try to move until we know what's wrong wit'cha!" the nasaly guy chuckled. Paul could see two men looking his way. One was tall, with broad shoulders and graying hair around the temples. The other one was shorter, slightly paunchy, and kept rubbing his nose with a handkerchief. *Nose Job Bob*, Paul laughed to himself.

The nose reminded him of... *The handkerchief.* Was it still in his pocket? All he remembered was reaching behind his back to retrieve the box. *Lillian will melt*, he had thought, *and then she'll apologize for kicking me out of the house. That box would say it all.* He scanned the interior of the ambulance. No sign of Lillian anywhere.

"Where's my wife?" he demanded.

"Do you mean Lillian Amadon?" Nasal Nose asked innocently.

"Of course that's who I mean. She's my only wife! Where is she?"

The two EMTs looked at each other, raising their eyebrows in some sort of secret code, Paul guessed.

"Sir, they had to take her into the station for questioning."

"The police station?"

"'Fraid so," the tall one said. The expression on his face signaled "Sorry," but Paul wasn't buying it. Kind of like when the doctors give you bad news and appear to be upset, but as soon as they leave the room they're yukking it up with the nurses.

"Look, we've had our differences lately..." Paul noticed the skeptical faces and added, "I guess that's an understatement. But guys, c'mon, are either of you married?"

Both men nodded. "Know how crazy your wives can get sometimes?" They nodded again and smiled knowingly.

"Well, Lil's no different, and I haven't been exactly a model husband. She didn't mean to hurt me. She must've thought I was so out of my gourd that I had a gun or something. But I swear, I've never even touched a gun, much less owned one!" The tall man sat down and the short one leaned against the ambulance wall. He could tell they were actually listening. *How long has it been since I talked and really let someone listen?*

Paul continued talking, and the men nodded politely and murmured their sympathies about his difficulties with work, the drinking, and now the problems with Lillian. By the end of the story, Paul could feel a tiny drop of water on his cheek. At first, he thought the ambulance had a leak. It took him a moment to recognize the tears that had become strangers to him over the past few years.

"So, you hit your rock bottom yet?" The tall EMT let the words sink in.

"Whaddya mean?"

"I mean, when someone has an addiction like you do – no offense, but ya do – things don't change until you hit rock bottom. Like, things can't get any worse, so you decide to clean up your act. Go to AA meetings, win back your wife's trust, that kinda stuff…"

Instead of lashing back with his usual sarcasm, he paused. Without a fresh infusion of alcohol, Paul allowed the sobering thoughts to penetrate his mind.

Ready to lose my job? Yep. Losing my wife? Yeah, may've already happened. Lost my house? Yessirree! I guess I'm as close to rock bottom as you can get.

"So… what do I do? Where do I go for help?" Another thought struck him. *How do I get Lillian out of trouble? The only reason she's at the police station right now is because of me. I never thought my drinking was hurting anyone. Guess I was wrong.*

"He's getting agitated," the Short One noticed. Paul could see them filling a syringe, and he knew that in a few short minutes, he wouldn't be talking or thinking clearly at all.

He cried, "Just tell my wife that I love her! Tell the police to let her go! It's not her fault I made her think I had a gun…"

His words trailed off as the medication did its job. Paul's eyes closed, and his head rolled lightly to the right side of the cheap ambulance pillow.

Both men looked at each other. "Poor guy. He's got a long road ahead of him."

"Yup," the other agreed.

The tall man looked thoughtful. "Think we should call the police? Let them know what he said?"

The other one shrugged. "Sure. Couldn't hurt, but y'know they'll probably figure the guy's delirious or something. He's definitely drunk, and who knows what else may be in his system?"

Randy, the tall EMT, picked up his cell phone and dialed. He spoke briefly to the front desk officer at the 38th precinct, answered a few questions, and hung up. He smiled at his fellow EMT.

"This Paul guy's gonna be happy when he comes to – they've already finished questioning his wife. Won't be allowed to see Paul for twenty-four hours, until the police get a statement from him, but at least he can rest easy knowing she's not in the slammer."

He remembered talking to the distraught woman and said, "Y'know, Ed, my mind isn't as sharp as it used to be, but I could swear I remember seeing that Lillian lady before tonight. Maybe at my wife's school? Or my daughter's? She looks awfully familiar, but I can't place her. Hmmm."

LILLIAN

Saturday 2:00 A.M.

Still shaking, Lillian walked to the front door. The officer held the screen door open. "You gonna be okay, ma'am?"

"Yes, I'm just a little shook up!" She tried to giggle but found that laughter would not come easily to her this evening. "Just tell me again – you're sure Paul's going to be okay?"

"Just fine, Ma'am, and as soon as the detective gets a statement from him, you're welcome to visit him at Centennial. I understand they had to sedate him, so in cases like this, no one may visit the person for at least twelve hours." He thrust a business card into her hand. "If you call sometime after noon tomorrow – I mean today, it's already Saturday – then they'll tell you when you may visit."

Lillian exhaled and smiled. This time, it was a true, genuine smile. *Paul's in good hands, he'll be okay, and I can visit him after the revival. Perfect timing!* "Thank you, Officer. For everything. I mean, I can't believe what happened, and…"

The officer interrupted, looking tired and worn. "Trust me, this kind of thing is more common than you can imagine, and if Paul's story matches yours, then it sounds like you were merely acting in self-defense. And if there's no lasting damage to your husband, well, then I guess everything will be okay." He turned to go.

Lillian called after him, "No lasting damage? Everything will be okay? Officer, do you really believe that's possible in life?"

He stopped briefly and turned back to face her. "Ma'am, I'd like to believe in happily-ever-after, but in my line of work, I've come to believe that those endings are best saved for movies and books."

He continued, rushing his words a bit, as if he were afraid to give her a chance to ask more questions. "Well, you take care of yourself, and remember, we're here 24/7 if you need us. G'night."

Lillian stood on the step as the officer ducked into the squad car and disappeared down the empty road. She replayed his final words in her head: *Saved for movies and books? How about a different kind of saving? If I can save others – do what Radio Rev says I must do – isn't all this trouble worthwhile?*

With that thought in her mind, she almost skipped into the house, anxious to see if the girls made it out of the house safely. A cursory look around the first floor reassured her that everything was just as she had left it.

She descended the stairs to the basement and stopped when she saw several unfamiliar items on the craft table. She walked over and read the note out loud: "Dear Miss Lillian, We are so sorry if we caused any of this mess. To make it up to you, we are going to try our best to get to your house by 5:30 tomorrow morning. We hope you make it home in time, since we have no way of driving to the revival without you. Here are our numbers if you need to text or call…"

She smiled, imagining how wonderful it would be to take the credit for saving someone's soul. *Make that two someones,* she thought giddily as she remembered that Karen would be going, too. She looked heavenward and said, "Lord, I never would have planned it this way, but who is to question Your methods?"

As she prepared for bed, she tried to push the nagging thought away. It was the one that seemed to resurface every night when she was crossing over from wide-awake consciousness to the relaxed state that would wash over her before drifting off to sleep. The words were different, but the message was always the same, and she didn't want to listen to that voice right now.

I'm too tired, she protested. *And I finally got what I – I mean what God and Radio Rev – wanted! Didn't I?*

But tonight, the voice was insistent. It was the voice that had warned her twenty years ago not to get on the bus the day it was raining. She had skipped the ride that day and later found out that bus had veered off the road following a slippery turn, plunging into the valley below, killing half of the passengers and the driver.

It was the same voice that, as a child, warned her about the other kids. That voice helped her realize that the ones who were superfriendly to her as they copied her homework but treated her like a leper the rest of the time were not to be trusted. And it was that voice that told her that until Paul wanted to quit drinking, she needed to stand firm and change how she related to him.

The voice was speaking again, and as she pulled the comforter up to her neck and relaxed the muscles in her body, she couldn't ward it off any longer. This time, the voice wanted to warn her about something different.

Lillian, look at you! You almost killed Paul. You were plotting to kidnap two innocent girls. You have completely changed your personality. And why? Why? How? When did this happen?

She turned to her side, but the voice was insistent tonight. *I'll tell you why. And I'll tell you when. When you started listening to that Radio Rev show. Because you wanted an easy answer, and that's what this guy's promising you. But every fiber of your being has been questioning it. You just keep letting everyone else's beliefs take precedence over your own!*

She flipped to her stomach and burrowed her head under the pillow, trying to hide from the words as she fell into a fitful sleep, full of disturbing, fiery images. Through the fire she could see an image of her younger self, wearing one of her favorite outfits – a purple tunic with flowing pants. Her long blonde hair was tied into a loose ponytail, and she wore glasses. She was sitting in a college classroom, and a younger version of Paul sat across from her. She continued to look down on her younger self, talking to Paul, laughing at his jokes. There was a sparkle in his eye and she touched his arm lightly as she asked him a question.

The comforting images evaporated, replaced by a dark fog. Something pulled at her feet. Whatever it was kept pulling, pulling…. dragging her down into an abyss. She cried out, but no one was there to help her. No one could save her.

A loud, buzzing noise filled Lillian's ears. She opened her eyes, feeling a dampness on her cheeks. She looked at the clock: 5:30 A.M. Then she heard it. A soft knocking. Three times. Then a pause. Then three knocks again.

She rushed to the window. Two shivering girls stood on the porch, looking at each other and shrugging their shoulders. Lillian tapped on the window. The faces looked up. She waved, they waved back, and she ran down the stairs, not even caring that she was still in her pajamas.

"Miss Lillian?" Hope started. "Are we still going? I mean, you're still wearing..." her words trailed off awkwardly. For a moment, she hesitated, thinking back to last night's dreams and the voice. Just as quickly, she pasted a smile on her face. *This decision was made months ago. I've gotta follow through.*

"Of course we're going!" Lillian shouted. "C'mon in, and I'll be ready in a jiffy!"

CHAPTER 24

Formula for Success

RADIO REV

Saturday 5:30 AM

"Good morning, listeners! It's a lovely day for a revival, isn't it?" The pre-recorded advertisement for WFAM filled Glenn's ears. He reached his arm out and hit the snooze button. He wanted to return to the dream that the annoying voice on the radio had just interrupted. Caroline was just getting ready to say that she missed Glenn and wanted to start over. In his dream, Glenn's heart felt fuller than it had in years – that is, until the alarm went off.

When he moved up North, he had convinced himself he was moving because of the job, but he knew in his heart there were plenty of offers in his hometown, and he just wanted to be closer to Caroline. And if he couldn't see her each day, he could do the second-best thing: read her daily column in the *Philadelphia Times*.

Apparently, Caroline's curiosity and strong opinions had served her well, for now she was the chief political correspondent for the paper. Every morning, Glenn would indulge himself in a cup of coffee and Section A: World News. There, he would drink in Caroline's opinions and commentary. Sometimes, he wasn't sure if it was the caffeine or her column that gave him his jump-start to the day.

After years of this morning routine, he discovered WFAM – and found it a much better way to block out the memories. Finally, he was so busy between his day job and the station that his time to think about Caroline decreased, until one day he noticed that he had forgotten to check the morning paper. Taking that as a good sign, he threw himself into his ministry even more. He pored over Bible verses, other successful evangelists' sermons, anything to make him a WFAM success. And successful he was.

He found that the sermon writing grew easier over time. Years before, when he had been a guest speaker at his dad's church, Glenn spent hours and hours deciding what to say, what he truly believed, and how those ideas intersected. Now, he didn't bother himself with his own opinions. No, it was much easier to parrot the messages similar to the other big-name religious personalities.

Glenn developed a simple formula: start with a Bible verse, explain the historical backdrop for the story and what Jesus (or Paul, or John – whoever was telling the story) meant. Then, bring that message to the present. Give a few real-life examples on how the verses apply to our modern-day lives. It worked especially well when he provided a humbling example from his own life to show that he was "just like" his listeners in their daily struggles. Then, he would move in for the kill – give some heartrending tear-jerker, ask for donations, and then cue the music! The combination of emotions and music created the desired effect – droves of loyal listeners who were more than willing to make a financial tithe to WFAM.

Lately, this recipe was becoming more and more successful. Maybe it was because more people than ever were losing jobs and looking for hope. Or maybe he had honed his craft like a well-oiled machine. Or…

Was it The Voice? The brainwashing?

He hated thinking about The Voice, so he simply ignored it and checked the clock instead. He was running late, a condition he loathed, so he busied himself with the pile of papers on his desk that he would need for the revival. In the bustle of running late, he forced the niggling feeling of guilt to return to its normal place – the back of his mind.

Guilt for what?

He had asked himself that question more than once. The answer was there, waiting in the wings like an actor ready to go on stage, but Glenn swiftly closed the curtains and walked out to his car.

CHAPTER 25

Pure Praise

HOPE

Saturday 5:30 AM

Somehow, Miss Lillian's house looked completely different by day. With the sun shining through the venetian blinds, the sparkling surfaces blinded us. My mother, not known for her housekeeping skills, would be so jealous of this clean house. Everything had a place. *Except for us. Where did we fit into this squeaky-clean picture?*

Not knowing where to stand or sit, I fidgeted from foot to foot. Miss Lillian didn't seem to notice our discomfort because all she said was how quickly she would be ready, and then she scurried upstairs.

I know that people get distracted, but c'mon! You just put us through an evening of hell! The least you could do is show some concern and a place to sit. I glared at the staircase and silently fumed.

A few minutes later, Miss Lillian bounded down the stairs, wearing an old favorite: long, teal skirt and matching top. *Good choice!* I congratulated her silently. Glad that we would be seen with Miss Lillian in her "old" clothes, I said, "Love the skirt, Miss Lillian!"

She looked down at the clothes, as if she hadn't put them on herself. "Oh? Thanks. Y'know, I haven't worn this for the longest time, but something made me feel like my old self again so I said, 'What the heck! Time for a little frivolity!'" I had no idea what frivolity was, but I wasn't sure if she was like a teacher when it came to definitions. *No need to ask now. I'll look it up later.*

"I'm so sorry, girls, I forgot to ask if you ate breakfast. Do you want me to stop on the way for something? Doughnuts? Bagels?"

There's that care and concern I was looking for! My stomach growled at the suggestion. I looked at Karen, an admitted doughnut fiend, and we smiled. "I guess a doughnut would be okay," Karen replied.

"Hope, doughnut's alright with you?"

I nodded in agreement. Sugary sprinkles and vanilla frosting would be absolutely perfect right about now. Besides, if we got caught, this would be my last supper, so to speak.

I thought back to our final minutes in the basement the night before. I don't know how we did it, but we had already managed some amazing feats in the past twenty-four hours. First, we snooped around Miss Lillian's house for a few minutes, wondering madly what Paul had pulled from his pocket. Karen grabbed the box and opened it. She gasped, "He's a romantic! Look…"

I peeked inside the box and shook my head. "What a shame. Just when he thought he might get a second chance, he got a blow to the head instead!" Karen nodded, and we decided the safest place for the box would not be on the floor but on the table with Lillian's art supplies.

Karen wondered out loud, "Is it okay to move evidence?"

I pondered that one for a moment and shrugged. "Probably not, but at this point, I think we've already broken most of the rules. What's one more?"

"Hope, you're starting to sound like me! What's gotten into you lately? Cursing, spying, basically saying f-you to the police and their investigation? Are you sure you're not an imposter?"

I smiled, figuring I'd tell Karen about *Finding Your Voice* later.

Karen wouldn't understand why I need a book to find myself. To her, it just comes naturally. Lucky!

The rest of our search at the Amadon residence proved that Lillian really was telling the truth – her house and life were totally, one hundred percent boring.

Besides escaping Miss Lillian's house undetected, we successfully invented a rather lame story about Karen not feeling well. My mom bought Karen's complaints that she would just feel better if she could sleep on her own bed with her high thread-count sheets. My mom probably didn't want to make Karen feel like a weirdo for requiring home goods to feel better, and she quickly allowed us to move the sleepover to the Pandora house.

Little did my mom know, but Karen's parents were out of town for the night. Sometimes, when all of the Pandora kids have overnight plans, Mr. and Mrs. Pandora celebrate by driving into the city for an expensive dinner and then they stay over in an upscale hotel. Last night was one of those rare occasions. Almost the second after I invited Karen over last week, Mrs. Pandora was on stayanight.com, lining up a good deal.

Sometimes, I felt kind of bad for Mrs. Pandora. *Life must be pretty grim if the moment your kids are away you feel the need to flee the area like an escaped prisoner.* However, based on the current situation, I was more grateful than ever for the Pandora staycation.

The night grew quiet once we settled in at Karen's, but I couldn't get used to the idea of being in the house alone with Karen. Sure, I had stayed by myself before, but tonight was different. Neither my parents nor Karen's had any idea that we were alone.

The five o'clock alarm was a welcome relief. It signified the beginning of the end of this nightmare. If these four hours could pass uneventfully, we would be in the clear. My conscience felt a little guilty, but I found I could brush it aside when I considered the consequences if anyone knew what we were up to. Plus, I was willing to do pretty much anything at this point to ensure that I got to see Eli later that evening.

So now here we were, loading ourselves into Miss Lillian's old car. Something about it felt vaguely familiar, but it wasn't until Karen started nudging me and madly pantomiming the old lady routine I did a few days ago that it made sense. I finally got it: *Lillian* was the person who was driving around Hidden Hills! *She must have been following me the other day!*

The car sputtered to life, and we watched trees, houses, and storefronts zip by. For an instant, a terrible thought struck me: *what if Miss Lillian is really some psychotic killer who used this whole revival thing to lure us into her car? And now she's going to take us to the woods and chop us into a million pieces. Or maybe she'll tie us up first, and torture us...*

I tried to dismiss the thoughts, but images of chainsaws, hockey masks, and blood filled my mind. Just as I was considering the physical damage of jumping out of a moving car, Miss Lillian slowed down. I peered out the smudgy window and saw a large tent in the middle of a parking lot. A huge "WFAM Family Radio Station" hung above the opening of the tent, and a winding line of people stood patiently outside of the structure. I breathed a sigh of relief.

"Here we are!" Miss Lillian sang. Gospel music filled the car as we opened the doors, and as we got closer to the line we could hear many of the line-waiters humming along. We found a spot in line while Miss Lillian ran across the street to the Donut World. She emerged from the shop carrying a large brown bag. She handed it to Karen. "While you wait," she smiled. I watched her small fingers wrap themselves around the large coffee cup she held in her left hand.

I surveyed the scene before me. Most of the people looked older than dirt, but I reminded myself that only old people and babies are crazy enough to be awake at such an hour. Many of the ladies wore large hats decorated with flowers and bows, and men and women alike were clutching Bibles to their chests like baby blankets. I couldn't tell if the frozen smiles on their faces were the result of sleep deprivation or if it was just a strange mix of people attempting to look friendly and polite.

A tall man appeared at the tent entrance. He introduced himself as the president of the station. "Good morning, everyone! Welcome to the Radio Rev Revival Weekend!" He was met with a warm round of applause. Karen and I followed along and clapped a few times. The man continued to talk, explaining how to enter the tent in an "orderly fashion" and how excited he was that so many people were willing to come out and worship this early in the morning. Karen nudged me and made a comment about how this guy acted like Mr. Vambles.

The man continued talking and chuckled, "I guess early rising's the least we can do to show the Lord how thankful we are for all of His blessings! Now, let's give a warm round of applause to our gospel band, Pure Praise…" I noticed that he had the same goofy grin on his face as the other worshippers.

The inside of the tent was immense. Mammoth Peavey speakers adorned the long, wooden stage. Flowers stood in bright vases, and more "WFAM" posters hung across the tent walls. Hundreds of folding chairs stood at attention like soldiers just waiting for us to occupy them. Miss Lillian took a quick look around and squealed, "Oh, good! Front row's still open!"

Front row? Even in school, the front row is never a good idea. That's the spot where you can't escape the teacher's stare, questions, or attention in general. I was sure this would be no different. We grudgingly sat next to Miss Lillian. Karen just looked around, eyes wide as ever. *Probably trying to figure out how to write this story without admitting she was here!*

I looked at my watch. 6:00 AM. Normally, the weekends fly by, and before I know it, Sunday night rolls around and I get those butterflies in my stomach about going back to school. Today was completely different. Time seemed to be going backward. Oh, well. There was nothing I could do except to enjoy the doughnut in my hand, so I chewed slowly and thoughtfully, hoping to make it last until the show began. *Let's get this over with.*

LILLIAN

Saturday 6:00 AM

Lillian felt giddy. *It's all working according to plan.* She truly believed it was worth the not knowing – not knowing if she would get Hope to the revival (she did!), not knowing if she was getting arrested (she wasn't!), not knowing if Paul would be okay (he would!). All of it was worth it.

Is this really worth it, Lillian? There it was again. That argumentative, doubting voice. It wasn't enough for that nagging voice to haunt her dreams. No, now that voice was following her around like a demanding puppy dog. The more she heard it, the more uncomfortable she felt about sitting in the folding chairs at the revival with two high school girls who were trying, unsuccessfully, to act as if this is how they spent every Saturday morning. The more she sat with her feelings, the more unnatural this felt – this changing of her life. Heck, she had changed the way dressed and spoke over the past few months!

Suddenly, Lillian missed Paul. Not the drunk, angry Paul, of course, but the Paul who was around most of the time. She even missed the pet peeves, like his annoying chewing, or the way he would leave all the laundry under the bed, only for her to discover it after she spent the weekend washing darks and lights. Yes, the good and the bad were parts of any marriage, but somewhere along the way she had decided that the only solution was to kick him out and get on with her life. *Though it's true that Paul needs to change, is there a possibility that I may need to change, too?*

Maybe that change doesn't involve revivals and radio pastors, either.

Even the soulful sounds of the guest band couldn't pull her from the thoughts. The more she allowed the feelings to flow through her, the more she felt as if warm rays of sunlight were penetrating through her body – a body which, lately, felt very cold. Empty. Even thoughts of Paul were warm. *How can pain feel warm?* she asked herself. But the answer came in a rush: *When you allow yourself to feel, it can all feel good. It's called being alive.*

She looked at the faces of the people sitting around her. Everyone was smiling, but something appeared plastic and unbelievable in their expressions. She wondered if the thoughts inside their heads were as empty as their grins. They were nodding, clapping, and saying amen at the appropriate times, but even that seemed staged. *Was everyone truly feeling the same way at the same time?* She doubted it.

Maybe it was the clothes. Maybe wearing her old, beloved outfit was shifting her perspective. Feelings of familiarity swept over Lillian. Like she was returning home – home to herself, a self that had been absent for a long time.

A jab in her ribcage jolted her. It was Karen. "Huh?"

"Miss Lillian, are you alright?" Before she could answer, Karen continued, "I was just asking you if I could have the extra doughnut."

Lillian laughed and tried to sound lighthearted. "Of course!" She fished the brown bag from her massive leather purse and handed it to Karen.

"Thanks!"

Lillian just nodded in response as a wave of nausea passed over her. The unrelenting voice returned, louder and clearer than ever:

Look at you, Lillian. These innocent girls risked getting into the biggest trouble of their lives. Why? For you. Because you had to save them. You know better. You know that you really just wanted to take credit for doing something important. Feeling like you're somebody. Paul's been telling you you're nobody, and you've believed it. Do these girls need saving? Who knows? But is it your business to force this on them? Who put you in charge of that kind of decision-making?

It was then that her body started shaking. At first, it was the uneasy feeling in her stomach. Then it turned into goose bumps, a slight chill and chattering teeth. She was afraid she was going to spill the hot coffee in her lap. She put the cup of steaming liquid on the floor and tried to calm down. *Take a deep breath,* she instructed herself.

The room spun, and everything lost focus. Somewhere, miles away, voices called her name. "Miss Lillian! Miss Lillian!" She tried to concentrate on a stationary object to ground herself but couldn't. The shaking turned violent, especially on the right side of her body. In a haze, she turned to the right. It was Hope, yanking her arm and asking, "Are you alright, Miss Lillian? You look a little pale."

If there was any doubt in her mind before, it was now gone. The voice was way too insistent to ignore. Lillian made another pivotal decision, but this one was entirely different from her earlier decision to take the girls to the revival. In one swift motion, she scooped up her coffee, slung her purse over her shoulder and announced, "Girls, let's get you out of here."

She paused, not sure how to explain herself. *An apology would be easiest.* "I'm sorry – for all of this. It was wrong to try to force you to go to the revival with me. That's not my decision to make." Each word lifted some of the heaviness she felt in her heart until she finally could breathe easily again. Now the smile on her face felt real.

The girls' faces revealed confusion and relief. Karen squealed with delight. "Thank God! I mean, thank YOU! Thank you, thank you, thank you! No offense, but this place gives me the creeps."

Through all of this, a family of three sat behind Lillian and the girls. With their colorless clothes and Stepford smiles, it was difficult to determine who was who, they looked so similar. The father tapped

Lillian on the cuff of her blouse. "Ma'am, you're blocking our view, so if you wouldn't mind taking your loud conversation elsewhere, I'd appreciate it." The whole time, the ridiculous smile remained on his face. He seemed to speak without moving his mouth, like a ventriloquist.

Lillian shot back, "Sir, I'm sorry you have to endure our 'loud conversation', but I do believe you can miss an amen or two! God will understand." She giggled.

The man's smile stiffened. "That may be, Ma'am, but you're interrupting my worship hour. I didn't come here to listen to some wild woman with her ill-behaved children and crackly bag of pastries punctuating my prayer!" His grin faded momentarily, but, as if the man realized the smile were disappearing, plastered it right back on that fake face of his.

A small boy sitting in between the man and woman shouted, "Yeah, beat it, Lady!" More sneer than smile covered his face, and the father whipped his head to the boy.

"Son, don't you speak to your elders like that! Let the adults handle this!"

Lillian laughed and threw her parting words over her shoulder. "Sir, if you're going to insult me, don't scratch your head when your child does the same! You know what they say about apples and trees. And sir?" She didn't wait for his reply. "Sometimes I think it would benefit us to let the kids speak their minds. They're more clear-headed than we can ever be."

She turned to the little boy and smiled. "Your father's right – telling me to beat it isn't very polite. But I forgive you. You're just being honest. Please remember to be honest for the rest of your life…even if hypocritical adults are telling you otherwise." She narrowed her eyes at the father.

The smile transformed into a smirk as the man hissed, "You leave my son alone. Stop filling his head with nonsense! Just be on your way before I report you to security!" Then, as quickly as he yelled at Lillian, he shifted back into his seat, grabbed his wife's hand, and rearranged his expression. The fake smile returned. It was clear that Lillian was now invisible to him. "Amen," he murmured, over and over.

As Lillian herded Karen and Hope through the throngs of people, Karen yelled, "You go, Miss Lillian!" Karen fist-pumped the air. Shocked and disapproving glances passed over the worshipers' faces. The trio neared the exit sign, and a man's voice boomed through the PA system.

It's Radio Rev! Lillian realized. *But something sounds different in his voice. Distorted, almost.* She looked to the stage to see this larger-than-life persona, but she quickly remembered he would be there "in words only". *How strange,* she thought. Lillian tuned into his sermon for a moment but the words sounded dead. Meaningless. For the first time, his message lacked the rhythm and song-like quality she was used to. *How did I miss that? Why did I think his words were so unique? So commanding?*

And then, she understood. The words of her counselor rang in her head: *Sadness and desperation can be best friends, and when loneliness enters the picture, watch out! That combination will destroy anyone in its path.*

Lillian continued to push her way through the people, saying "Excuse me!" as she passed, but very few people willingly let her through without giving her a dirty look that disguised itself as a grin. Four people blocked the exit, and the first thing Lillian noticed was that they did not wear smiles on their faces. In fact, they weren't making any attempt to look happy, which caused Lillian to light up with relief. *Real people!*

Before anyone could enjoy the reality-check, Karen walked toward one of the door-blockers. She opened her mouth and squawked, "Mom?"

HOPE

Saturday 6:15 AM

I had just finished my doughnut when Miss Lillian grabbed us and told us we were leaving. Something in her eyes looked vaguely familiar. *I know...it's the way she looked when we first met her.*

Confused but thankful, I remained silent. If she was going to get us out of here, the less said the better. I wouldn't want her to change her mind. The sooner we could leave, I reasoned, the sooner we could get back to Karen's and get on with our lives.

I looked around the room. People were swaying in time with the music, and every now and then a few would shout out, "Amen!" and, "Preach it to me!" The first time someone did that, I held my breath. At Roosevelt, if you called out, you would get yelled at. Or, the teacher would stop, and during an embarrassingly long silence, stare you down until you melted into your seat, wishing you had an invisibility power that would kick in. But no one here told anyone to stop, and the more often people shouted out, the more the others joined in.

The scene before me contrasted sharply with any other church I had visited. The people I was used to seeing were super-serious about religion, and I couldn't picture any of them randomly shouting out, no matter how good the preacher or music was!

Once, when I was nine or ten, I had asked my mom why we didn't go to church. Her answer was surprisingly short, considering Mom's long-windedness: "I don't have anything against God, but I think you need to make that decision when you're older. Just live your life following the Golden Rule, and you'll be doing what every religion asks you to do, anyway."

The three of us stood up, and now Miss Lillian and a man were trading arguments with one another. *Go, Miss Lillian!* I thought. Karen even said it out loud, and the man and his bratty son looked completely baffled as we exited the tent. Other people we passed had stone smiles on their faces. *How can a smile be stony?* I wondered. But that was the only word to describe it.

The red exit sign flashed like an oasis in the desert, and my feet picked up speed. *Almost home!*

I looked towards the exit again and squinted, figuring my eyes were playing tricks on me. *It can't be!* Four people stood in the doorway, looking surprisingly familiar. As we got closer, I heard Karen yell.

Oh, no. *Did she just say Mom?*

Now I could clearly see them: Mom, Dad, and Mr. and Mrs. Pandora. All four of them looking eerily identical at the moment – furious.

CHAPTER 26

Authenticity 101

RADIO REV

Saturday 6:15 AM

It's time, he thought to himself. *After today's service.*

He thought again of the dream that he couldn't shake. The dream of Caroline. *What would she think of me now? I'm not at all like the Glenn she once knew.*

Between oversleeping, rushing to get ready, and in general, being in a brain fog, Glen walked into the tent almost thirty minutes late. As station manager, he knew it was Suzanne's job to make sure he got to the revival on time, but he could care less about the dirty look she gave him as he swooped into the booth where he would speak. All he wanted to do was get on with the sermon and then hop in his car. *And drive where?*

He had longed to contact her, but something always stopped him. The one time he had finally convinced himself to follow through with his plan – keys in one hand, directions scribbled on a Post-it – the phone rang.

It was his dad, congratulating him on his most recent sermon. "Top-rated religious show in the Northeast, eh, Son? You've done me proud."

The keys fell from Glenn's hand, and after he hung up the phone, he crumpled the Post-it note, knowing it wouldn't happen that day, either. And on and on. Fifteen years of false starts. Fifteen years of almost stalker-like behavior. Several reckless drives to the *Philadelphia Times* office, where he sat in his car like a coward just to watch her walk down Market Street. He never made contact with her, but he spent hours digging through the internet like an archaeologist, combing for facts from her personal life.

Married? Once, briefly. For a year, right out of college. Quickie marriage, quickie divorce, and from what he could see, no other marital blemishes. Living quarters? Two-bedroom in Bala Cynwd. Close enough to the city to have a pulse on Philadelphia, yet suburban enough to feel safe living alone. Personal life? A few close girlfriends. Two dogs. Hobbies? Yoga and jogging. From years of research, he felt he knew her better now than he did in high school.

The day his father called to congratulate him on the accomplishment of the "Top-Rated Religious Show in the Northeast," Glenn knew why he was working so hard for WFAM. For so many years, he was looking for encouragement and acceptance. It would go something like this: *Glenn, we're proud of you. Glenn, you're okay with us! Glenn, we love you for you, no matter what. Glenn, you're Somebody.*

His dad's phone call that day was a milestone – the first time anyone told him he was good enough. And with every sermon and chart-topping donation report, Glenn had almost convinced himself that this Somebody was the person he was meant to be.

He stood in the booth and cleared his throat, thinking about the thousands of people who were attending the revival. Knowing he was well-liked felt incredible, but he still wondered, *Am I really happy?*

If Caroline were part of my life, I might be genuinely happy for the first time ever.

With that, he began his sermon. He knew he sounded different. He purposely didn't use The Voice, and he even forgot to quote the scripture at the right time. He toned down his southern accent, the accent he only revealed while preaching. It had been just one more way he had been able to keep work and WFAM separate.

No one had ever realized the connection between The Voice on the Philadelphia radio station and the voice of a principal from a school just a few short miles across the bridge in New Jersey. Radio Rev of WFAM? Principal Glenn Vambles of Roosevelt High?

One and the same.

Today, speaking from the heart, Glenn's message sounded simple, almost child-like. Certainly not as difficult as he made it sound over the past three years. Gone was the voice roll, and without using the "mind reform" techniques, he wondered what effect he was having on his listeners.

He listened to himself as he spoke into the microphone: "Let your life speak." As those words rolled off his tongue, he tried to remember where he heard them. *Who had said that?*

Caroline, of course. She had been quoting a famous Quaker. *What's a Quaker?* he had asked, and she had laughed and told him that Quakers were simple people who believed in the light within – or "the good" – that existed in everyone.

Wow, he thought. *Good within everyone? Guess that's a little different from the hard-hitting sermon I had planned for today.*

He turned off the mike. Suzanne rushed to his side. "Is that it, Rev? You're only at twenty-five minutes." He was supposed to speak for forty, and then the money collections would begin.

She looked at him desperately. "What about the Bible verses? The testimonials? That sad story about the sick woman who tuned in and turned her life around?"

Glenn stared blankly at his manager. Suzanne added, "Seriously, Rev. You've gotta give them a little more. I know this service is the free one and all, but that doesn't mean you can't give them a few more minutes of your time!" She tapped her pen on her clipboard, waiting for his response.

Glenn had no more time, though. He wasn't going to chicken out again.

"Suzanne, let them give what's in their hearts. I don't need to tell these people what to do. They're big boys and girls. Let them decide." And he rushed out of the tent without another word.

Apparently, though, he *did* need to tell the people in the tent what to give, for when the day was over and the money was counted, the collections accounted for less than half of what the station normally made on one of Glenn's tirades.

People could be heard grumbling as they left the tent. "Pure Praise was incredible, but in person, Rev just wasn't the same. Hmmm…." And their questioning comments drifted through the air like floating feathers.

Glenn didn't hear any of it, though. Even if he had, he wouldn't have minded. All he cared about was getting in his car and merging onto route 76, headed for the Walt Whitman Bridge. He exited at Route 1: "City Line/Bala Cynwd." He held his breath, gripped the wheel, and put on the turn signal. The GPS voiced its robotic commands and recalculated until the gleaming apartment building came into view.

The modern, mostly-glass high-rise boasted a security guard and buzz-in entry. Glenn knew he didn't have the code, so he pressed the visitor's button. A gruff voice from the other end answered. "May I help you?"

"Yes, I'd like to see, uhh, Caroline Richards. Room 312."

"May I ask who is calling?"

"Just tell her Glenn would like to see her."

"And does Glenn have a last name?"

He thought for a moment and then answered, "Just say Glenn. She'll know."

He could hear the man chuckling before he said, "Alright, Just-Say-Glenn, let me page her."

A minute later, a loud buzzer vibrated above and the front door automatically swung open. Glenn stepped inside and looked around. More glass, lots of green plants, and geometric artwork decorated the contemporary lobby. From his research, Glenn knew that many of Philadelphia's elite lived in this building: politicians, news anchors, even celebrities who shot movies in Philadelphia were known to set up temporary residences here. Thankfully, Glenn thought, the atmosphere felt welcome, not snobbish. Friendly, not judgmental. *Nonjudgmental, unlike me.*

He sighed. *I hope she can forgive me for all the years I've put the world's opinions above my own. And hers.*

HOPE

Saturday 6:20 AM

Oh, no. The moment of truth. This could get ugly. These and other terrible clichés streamed through my head. Only this wasn't some movie where the hero goes down in flames, only to be rescued later. This was real life, and *I* was the main character. And I was the one going down in flames. Or at least, getting punished for a very long time.

We were gathered around my parent's SUV, sorting out what happened. It wasn't easy. Four worried parents who can interrupt conversations under normal conditions were even more difficult to keep focused on the events of the past twenty-four hours. Questions volleyed through the air like ping pong balls, and sometimes I fell silent, knowing that Karen would answer for me. Then I could just listen and worry about my punishment in silence.

"What in God's name would possess you two to sneak out of the house to spy on someone?" That one was from my mom. Karen did a decent job of explaining her dreams of becoming the next Missy Chang. As she spoke, the Pandoras' faces turned red, but I couldn't tell if it was from anger or embarrassment.

Mr. Pandora yelled, "Karen Lynn, that is the most ridiculous reason I've ever heard! A reporter? You want to be a reporter?"

How could he not know that little tidbit of information? He didn't even let her respond. "Well, you can report on the longest grounding in the history of mankind, because you'll get to experience it firsthand!" Even my parents, who usually thought the Pandoras were over-the-top with punishments, were nodding in agreement.

Miss Lillian broke in. "Mr. and Mrs. Minor, Mr. and Mrs. Pandora, please. Please remember these girls were just being kids, and they got mixed up with a complicated situation. They were just trying to help me by coming back today to go to the revival. If you want to be upset with someone, it should be me."

With that, all eyes turned to Miss Lillian and the inquisition began: How could she knowingly take two girls away from home? How could she allow them to sneak out of the house, fully aware they were lying to their parents? And, for that matter, how could any responsible adult allow those girls to sneak back home on a Friday night and not tell their parents what happened? And…just how much had the girls seen and heard at the Amadon household?

I looked at Karen in horror. *Here it comes,* I thought. *Now my dad will go berserk.*

"They saw everything, Sir," Miss Lillian answered quietly.

"Saw? What do you mean, saw?"

For once, I wished Karen hadn't answered this one. "She means that after Miss Lillian hit Paul…I mean, Mr. Amadon, we were in the closet when you and the police arrived."

My father's face seemed to inflate to twice its size. "You mean they saw you strike your husband, and they witnessed our rescue effort?" The anger I was sure would be directed at me was now focused on Miss Lillian.

"Sir, I have to say, your daughter behaved heroically. While we were frozen with fear, your daughter snapped into action and checked Paul's vitals. She was the one who knew he was still alive but needed medical attention as quickly as possible. I'm amazed at her composure and maturity."

For a moment, I thought Dad's face softened when he looked my way. "Really?" His voice didn't have the sharp edge from a moment before. He coughed and resumed his lecture. "Well, even though I'm glad that Hope was helpful, I still can't believe our girls were witnesses to this, and that you didn't tell me or the police that there were other people in the house! You made a statement to the police last night, and you left out those details? What were you thinking?"

No one answered that one. I've never claimed to know what other people think, let alone a crazy woman who just whacked her husband with a bat and then forced the witnesses to attend a religious service the next day. Miss Lillian was at a loss for words.

Karen tried changing the subject, and I had to admire her bravery, because this technique usually works with our parents. Today, however, her attempt took us in the wrong direction. "So, how did you find us?"

Now it was Mrs. Pandora's turn to rant. About how my mom called to see how long Hope and Karen were staying at the Pandoras' house. And how Mrs. Pandora told Mom that we were at their house, not the Pandora's because they were in Philly. And how they had to cut short their night in the city to see why we were at the Pandora's house alone, God forbid. And how they had to rush out of the hotel (couldn't even enjoy the free buffet breakfast!). And how they almost got a ticket on the Schuylkill Expressway driving eighty miles an hour. And how when they got home, all they found in the house were two unmade beds and a digital camera. And how they looked at the pictures Karen took. And how they showed my parents the pictures. And how Dad recognized the Amadon basement from the night before. And how they rushed to Miss Lillian's house and almost got another ticket for driving down Vista View Road at fifty miles an hour. And how they got to Miss Lillian's bungalow, ran inside (door was unlocked!) and found the flyer for the WFAM event. And how they actually did get a ticket driving to the revival at eighty miles an hour again (and now the Pandora car insurance rates are sure to be raised... *Do you know how expensive that will be, girls?*). And finally, how they still couldn't believe their eyes when they saw us walking towards them at the revival with the Roosevelt High School secretary leading the way.

"Oh." Karen's usually sparkling, inquisitive eyes turned dark and flat. *Change-the-subject strategy? Epic fail.*

Dad broke the silence. "Well, I think Detective McGroarty will enjoy hearing this story, don't you, Lillian?" He grabbed my hand and walked me around to the other side of the car. "Get inside, Hope. Karen, get in your parents' car. We need to talk to Miss Lillian. Alone."

I peered out the window, trying hard to look like I wasn't staring and spying on them. But I don't think they would have noticed, anyway. Even through the closed car door, I could hear several voices speaking at once, the occasional high-pitched voice of Mrs. Pandora, and the deep voices of our dads. They weren't exactly yelling, but I was glad to be inside the car and not the target of their wrath.

For a moment, I almost felt sorry for Miss Lillian. She looked as if she were melting into the colorful fabric she wore that day, and her normally rosy complexion looked pasty and dull. She lowered her head, and I could see the small crops of gray roots from her scalp contrast with the dyed hair that hung over her shoulders.

After several minutes, she shuffled over to her car, opened the door, and got inside. She put her head in her hands, resting her elbows on the steering wheel. My dad strode over to her car and knocked on the window. Miss Lillian jumped, looked through the glass at my dad, and scrambled in her purse for something. A second later, I could see the white reverse lights appear at the back of her car. The dilapidated sedan slowly backed out of the parking spot and disappeared down the road.

I held my breath, waiting for my parents to open the car doors and start in on me. When they got in the car, however, they just sat there. I looked at the backs of their heads. I could see part of my mom's profile. One small tear slid down her cheek. The tear dropped off her jaw line and made a dark spot on her lavender blouse. My dad's shoulders kept rising and falling, like he was going to suck up all the oxygen in the car.

I had been silent long enough. "Mom? Dad?" Neither responded. "Please hear me out. I'm so, so sorry about what happened. Believe me – Karen and I never, in a gazillion years, expected this to happen. I was just so tired of always being such a goody-goody, and when we heard that Miss Lillian had a church in her basement, we wanted to find out what she was talking about. Honest, that's it. If we ever knew what was going to happen, we wouldn't have done any of this! I know it was wrong, but please understand! I just wanted to be a rebel for once."

My dad laughed. A good sign. "Well, you were rebellious alright! Good job on your only time of breaking all the rules. You certainly went all the way!"

I smiled, but I knew his laugh didn't mean everything was okay. "I know you guys are disappointed in me, and I'm sorry we got in the way of your rescue effort. If we hadn't been in the house, maybe Miss Lillian's husband wouldn't have seemed so threatening to her. She was only trying to protect us, you know."

The anger returned. "She has a funny way of being protective, Hope. Don't try to make her sound like the hero. She's the adult, and what she did was wrong on so many levels, I don't even know where to begin!"

I guess he figured out where to begin, though, because for the next twenty minutes, we drove around in what seemed like endless circles while Dad detailed every one of Miss Lillian's transgressions and how any decent, responsible adult wouldn't have done a single one of those things, much less all of them!

Finally, Dad turned into Hidden Hills. The same tree-lined streets, the same houses I had known all my life. Yet today, everything looked different – wrong and out of place. He maneuvered the car into the driveway, and turned off the ignition. We sat in the car, silent, for several minutes. *Do I get out? Go to my room? Stay here?*

My mom spoke. Her voice sounded gravelly, like she just woke up and needed a drink of water. "Hope, please go to your room. Your father and I need to discuss this."

Uh, oh. When Mom speaks that calmly and needs time to think and discuss something, it's serious. I heard this line too many times before, but it was usually intended for Patrick, not me. I also knew from those discussions that the consequences between both of them were far worse than whatever one of them cooked up alone. Another vocabulary word popped into my head: synergy. The sum is greater than its individual parts. *Yes, Mom and Dad's joint punishments had way too much synergy.*

I walked through the house slowly, trying to savor the sights and sounds as I made my way towards my room. The TV, the warm kitchen with its dark wood cabinets and inviting granite countertops. Even the upright piano sitting in the living room, the one I tried to procrastinate practicing on. All of these items looked precious, knowing that I might not be seeing the rest of the house for a long time. I walked into my room, and settled in on my bed.

This, I thought, would be home. I pulled my cell phone out of my purse and said a silent goodbye to it. I shoved my backpack off the bed with my foot, and as it thumped on the floor I said a mental goodbye to the iPad inside. Whenever Pat got grounded, all of the amenities of the bedroom would be stripped, leaving only clothes and books.

I looked over at my bulging bookshelves. *At least I'll get a lot of reading done. Ms. Tievel will be happy.* Images of baseball bats and prison bars wafted through my mind as I drifted off into a light, fitful sleep, waiting for my parents to come upstairs and deliver their verdict.

LILLIAN
Saturday 7:00 A.M.

It was time. *Time to take responsibility for my actions. Isn't that what I kept demanding from Paul?* In the back of her mind, she knew that her lies to the police would come back to haunt her, and her omissions about Hope and Karen being witnesses would need to be told, but another part of her thought that somehow, some way, this might all blow over. The delusional part of her, she realized.

For the second time in twenty-four hours, she walked into the imposing brick structure. The police station was a quick drive from the WFAM revival. *Too quick,* Lillian thought. She hardly had time to compose her thoughts before the irritable-looking secretary looked Lillian up and down and grumbled, "Can I help ya?"

"Uh, yes. I'm here to see Detective McGroarty."

The secretary snapped her gum as she dialed the detective's extension. Lillian stared at the red fingernails on her hand in order to prevent herself from glaring at the secretary, whose attitude seemed to say, "How dare you make me pick up this phone!"

"Mac? There's a lady here to see ya … name?" In a bored voice, she mumbled, "Name, Ma'am?"

Lillian wasn't sure she heard the woman. "You want my name?" For that apparently stupid question she wasn't even granted the honor of a reply, so she simply stated, "Lillian Amadon."

The secretary motioned to an orange vinyl chair. Lillian sat on the edge of the seat and hoped the detective wouldn't make her wait too long. She wanted to get this over with. The guilt and uncertainty about what would happen next made her hands sweat. She hid her hands so the secretary wouldn't notice.

After a few minutes of waiting, a large, ruddy-faced man appeared in the doorway, wearing a smile. Lillian prayed he would maintain that upbeat attitude for what she was about to tell him.

"Hello, there." He held out his hand. "Mac McGroarty. What may I do for you today?" His face still looked cheerful and warm.

"I, uhh, was here last night, talking to Officer Conlan. There was a, umm, ahh … domestic dispute in my house, but there were a few details I didn't get to share that might be kind of important."

Mac raised his eyebrows with interest. He motioned for Lillian to accompany him down the long corridor to his office. The walk felt like the one a prisoner would take during the days of pirates. *Walking the plank*, Lillian thought as she marched behind the detective and squeezed into the small office of his at the end of the lengthy hallway.

She didn't even give him a chance to sit before launching into her story. Coming clean, sharing everything from her loneliness when she made Paul leave, to finding comfort in Radio Rev's daily sermons, felt cleansing. The detective madly scribbled notes on a yellow legal pad. When she got to the part about Hope and Karen stumbling into her basement and Paul's intrusion, Mac stopped her.

He left the room. Lillian could hear muffled voices talking outside the door. She peered through the glass window on the door. It was the officer from last night. Officer Trevor. *Probably trading notes on all of my stories*, Lillian thought glumly. The two men entered the office and asked Lillian to recount the Friday night timeline. Both remained silent until the point in the story where she pressured the girls to return the next day, or else.

"Or else what?" Mac's expression had turned from friendly to suspicious.

"That I would tell their parents about sneaking out to spy on me." She looked from Trevor to Mac. Stony expressions met her pleading eyes. She began to sob. "I only wanted to help them! Save them," she cried.

Mac asked, "Save them?"

Lillian tried to explain Radio Rev's Save-A-Soul campaign, but she was sure her explanation made little to no sense. She looked at each officer. Though she couldn't be sure, she thought she noticed a glimmer of understanding that seemed to flicker deep in Officer Trevor's eyes. *Did he believe me? Could he understand how crazy I've felt lately?*

"Is that all?" Mac asked. She nodded and lowered her head with remorse.

Now it was Trevor's turn. "Mrs. Amadon, thank you for coming in here today."

Lillian looked up with anticipation. "So I can go now?" her voice rose with excitement. She stood up.

The two men exchanged knowing glances. Officer Trevor spoke again. "Not quite."

Mac took over again. "Lillian, I know that coming here today must have been difficult for you, and the fact that you came to us instead of the other way around will make your life a whole lot easier." He paused, as if what he was about to say next wouldn't be easy or pleasant.

"Unfortunately, what you've described is a form of blackmail. And you blackmailed two underage children. Though I've got some more questions for you, I think the next person you need to talk to is our psychiatrist. That will determine the direction this case takes. In the meantime, I will need to read you your rights."

And before she knew what was happening, Lillian heard them read her Miranda rights as the iron handcuffs encircled her wrists. Teardrops fell onto the cold metal shackles as Officer Conlan led her out of the cramped office and down the long hallway, but this time they escorted her to the temporary holding cell.

The last thing she saw was Detective McGroarty picking up the phone. The last thing she heard was Mac's voice asking the sour secretary to find the WFAM phone number. The last thing she felt was the stony bed that caught her. If anyone would have walked by the small cell, they would have been greeted with a woman, unconscious from the sheer stress and exhaustion of her life, curled up on the prison cot, her bright clothing providing sharp contrast to the grey nothingness of the jail cell walls.

RADIO REV

Saturday 8:00 AM

The elevator doors opened. Glenn held his breath. A thirty-something woman with dark hair stepped out and walked toward him. Her small stature belied the larger-than-life personality she managed to transmit to her readers with her powerful words now published daily in eight major cities. For a moment, everything around Glenn started to spin. He couldn't believe that after all these years, he had finally summoned the courage to make contact with Caroline.

"Glennie!" Caroline squealed, running toward Glenn, arms open to embrace him.

Too choked up to speak, he welcomed the hug and smelled the sweet scent from her glossy hair. He coughed, gathered himself together, and mumbled, "It's great to see you, Caroline. It's been too long."

He gazed into her eyes, looking for clues to gauge her reaction. Was she surprised? Excited? Or just being polite to an old boyfriend?

"It *has* been too long! How are you, Glenn?" She smiled, and all the years of inner turmoil faded in Glenn's mind. *If only I could see that smile every day… everything would be alright.*

A knot formed in his stomach. *What if Caroline had listened to my broadcasts?* Glenn shuddered with the knowledge that everything he had been preaching up until today was more of the same from the hometown that practically shunned this amazing woman. None of his sermons would endear Caroline to him. If anything, they would push someone like Caroline away.

Someone like Caroline. What did that mean? Someone kind. Someone loving. Someone tolerant. Open-minded.

Caroline motioned for Glenn to walk with her. Seemingly unaware of Glenn's overwhelmed state of mind, she suggested, "Let's grab a coffee." The two walked out of the building and across the street to the local coffee house. They sat down on a green couch and ordered two cappuccinos.

With the questioning and listening skills of a trained journalist, she patiently learned about the last fifteen years of Glenn's life – the trek to the North, his rising popularity with the radio show, the approval of friends and family, even the long sickness and death of his grandmother. He was ready to mention the secret that had catapulted him to fame in the religious radio sector, but something made him hold back.

Don't give away too much. Not yet. He paused.

Caroline smiled, but something lingered behind her dark lashes. A shadow from the past. A question hung in the air, and Glenn knew he couldn't ignore it any longer. He had to explain those final actions of his, those cutting words from high school. The break-up.

"I couldn't stand having the whole town hate me, disapprove of me. Or reject you. And I was so scared that when you went off to college that you'd meet someone smarter than I was. Someone who would sweep you off your feet! You'd figure I was just a small-town boy. You would let me go, I was sure of that, and I had too much pride to let that happen. So, I pushed you away. That's why I broke up with you."

The truth will set you free. Glenn felt the heaviness in his chest melt away as he finally unburdened himself to the person who needed to hear his words the most.

She finally spoke, almost whispering, "You thought I was going to find someone better? That's why you started that argument? Broke up with me because…?"

Her voice trailed off. Glenn nodded and looked down at his feet. For once, his oratory skills took leave of him. He waited patiently for Caroline's response, and with each passing second steeled himself for the rejection he so adamantly fought off years before.

It's was Caroline's turn. She spoke of those misfit years of being the black sheep of an entire town. "When you broke up with me, I knew I had no choice but to make a clean break. You were the only one there who had accepted me for who I was. At least, accepted me while we were dating. It was hard to believe you would have changed so quickly, but who knew?" She looked at her tiny hands that clutched the porcelain mug. She glanced at Glenn and added, "But I never hated you."

Glenn brightened. *I never hated you.* Had he been wrong, spending years and years agonizing over a single mistake?

Could it be this easy? It was time to forge ahead. Glenn coughed nervously. "So, maybe we can pick up where we left off?"

This time Glenn refused to look away. He watched every move, prepared to listen to every nuance in her voice. Caroline's hands shook, and she carefully returned the mug of coffee to the table before she spoke. He held his breath, wanting to hear the words he had waited for…

"Glenn, I'm…"

PAUL

Saturday 8:00 AM

Lights shined brightly into Paul's face. He rubbed his eyes. Even almost-motionless blinking caused excruciating pain over his temple. This morning the pain wasn't quite as intense as it had been the night before.

Thank God, he thought. The doctors assured Paul that the blow to his head did little damage. "You're lucky you have such a thick skull," the doctor concluded, "or else the injury could have been far worse – maybe even fatal."

Paul knew he was hard-headed, but finding out it was true, literally, made him think, *I've been thick-headed my whole life; so how is it that my way is the best way if I'm without a house, an estranged wife, and a drinking problem?*

There. He finally did it. Admitted to himself that his drinking had turned into a problem. *Isn't that the first step?* The doctor assured him that it was, and Paul already made plans to admit himself to Re-Vitalize, a local rehabilitation center for people with addictions. He knew if he didn't do it now, he may never do so.

He heard that Lillian had called the hospital last night and expressed relief with the news that Paul's damage wasn't permanent. Even though Lillian was the one who landed him in the hospital, he knew it was the drinking that led them both down this path.

After the initial anger wore off and he stopped hosting a pity party for himself, Paul knew that Lillian was still the love of his life. No matter what lay ahead, he would do whatever it took to win a place in her heart again.

He heard a soft knock on the door. The nurse who took Lillian's call poked her head into the room. "Paul?" she asked. "You have a phone call. It's your wife. She says she needs to talk to you, that she's tied up and can't visit you at the moment."

She patched the call through to the phone next to Paul's hospital bed. Even talking hurt his head.

Paul whispered, "Hello?"

CHAPTER 27

Seeking Forgiveness

RADIO REV

Now it was Caroline's turn to look uncomfortable.

She began again. "Glenn, I'm flattered to know you've been thinking of me all these years, but you have to understand how hurtful you and everyone in Mountwell were to me."

He stared at her, on the edge of the couch now, hoping against hope that he was not hearing her correctly.

"And even though I don't hate you, what you did…" her voice caught for a moment. "What you did was almost impossible to forgive."

"Almost impossible?" He hung onto each word as if it were a life preserver, ready to rescue his heart.

Caroline nodded. "Yes, almost impossible to forgive – but not completely. What I've realized is that if I hadn't left that town as fast as I could… if I had held on to my resentment to the people of Mountwell, or held onto you…"

She smiled, but Glenn winced. She didn't seem to notice, for she was staring up at the ceiling as if it held all the answers to her past and present.

"I didn't know this at the time, but I wouldn't be the person I am today if it weren't for you and everyone else in that small-minded place! Sure, if we would have stayed together, I would have been happier at the time. And I would've studied journalism and pursued my writing career. But, Glenn, it was the pain – the raw pain that only a true heartbreak can deliver – that drove me to work harder than anyone else. I truly believe that those dark days became the key to my success! More importantly, those hurtful years forced me to find out who I truly am. And to trust my instincts. You know, distinguish between authentic people and fake…" Her eyes opened wide as she considered her audience.

Glenn raised his eyebrows, waiting for more. Caroline took the hint and added, "Your breaking up with me taught me so much. It has allowed me to experience the power of forgiveness, and I do mean it when I say I forgive. But…"

"But?"

"But I can't forget what happened."

Glenn finally looked away as Caroline took another deep breath and sighed. "Listen, I appreciate your confession, your honesty, but everything between us happened years ago! Even you must have known that we are two very different people…?"

The shocked look on Glenn's face startled Caroline. *He must know all of this, right?* "Glenn, this can't come as a surprise to you. I'm a different person now, and even though I don't know much about your radio show, I'm sure you're a different person, too, especially after all these years, and…"

She stopped again. *He really wants to get back together. Doesn't he get it? We're not in high school anymore.*

But Glenn got the point.

Fifteen years later, there's no escaping the inevitable.

A pained look crossed his face. Caroline added, "But, Glenn, think about the lessons we've learned from this! We're better people now. We know more. Isn't that what matters?"

No. He couldn't speak. That single word kept repeating itself. *No, no, no…*

What had felt like sun shining in his heart earlier that day switched off. Half dream, half hope, Glenn had started to believe it might be that easy: Caroline may have simply felt the same way about him, even after all these years.

But no. He was the fool, finally forced to listen to the goodbye speech he had dreaded and prevented from his teens. Now, the day of reckoning had arrived.

She won. *She got to say no to me. Caroline got to call things off. No matter how hard I tried, in the end, it happened. She broke my heart.*

PAUL

Lillian's voice filled his ears, along with a profuse apology about not being able to visit him that morning. She told him about the revival and the girls' parents showing up. She mentioned the previous evening's events. "Paul, I only hit you because I thought you had a gun!"

Paul smiled for a moment, but even that small facial movement caused the intense pain to return. "Lil, I may have a quick fuse, but I thought you knew me better than that! I don't know the first thing about guns, much less how to shoot one." It was then that he told her about the box in his back pocket that held the earrings. "You've always wanted diamond earrings. I was going to make your wish come true."

Lillian didn't answer, but based on the choked-up noise she made, he could imagine her eyes must have been filled with tears.

"But I have no idea where those earrings are now. They're probably on the floor of the basement. Or one of those EMT's might have taken a souvenir. Who knows?"

Lillian spoke with determination. "Paul, no matter what happens, I want you to know I love you. I've told you before, but I'll tell you again – I want you back home, but only when you're sober. It's because I love you that I made you leave."

And at long last, he believed her. A question niggled in the back of his mind as she spoke, but he wasn't thinking clearly enough to bring it to his conscious awareness. He promised her that he would do whatever it took to get better. They hung up, and Paul fell back into an exhausted sleep.

When he awoke, Paul remembered something Lillian had said. What did she mean, "no matter what"? Hadn't they been through the worst already? If he's getting treatment, don't things go uphill from here? What *wasn't* Lillian telling him?

He thought about his questions all day, during the doctor's rounds, during the bland breakfast. During the bland lunch later that day, and during the bland Saturday afternoon television shows in his room. It wasn't until a man in a suit wielding a detective's badge entered the room that the numbness wore off. *I guess it's time to get the answers to my questions.* Paul tried to sit up, but the agonizing pain returned. He let his head fall back onto the hospital pillow.

He just nodded and listened to Detective McGroarty explain the reason for his visit: his wife had just turned herself in for blackmail and for endangering the welfare of minors. She was being held in a cell at the Lost Oak Municipal Building.

Paul knew his role would be pivotal during the questioning. If he came across as a hapless victim, then Lillian's problems were sure to get worse. Much worse. But, if Paul made every effort to cast Lillian in a positive light, he could help, not hurt, her cause. The memory of the baseball bat in her hands flashed through his brain. *This must be the "no matter what" Lillian mentioned... that she loves me no matter what. Do I feel the same?*

He took a deep breath and knew what he had to do.

CHAPTER 28

Name-Changer

RADIO REV

She broke my heart. She broke my heart....

The phrase replayed itself like an iPod on a hateful repeat mode. Mentally, he turned off the repetitive track and made a decision. Yes, the decision was a bit forced, but Glenn was a pro at fooling others. And an expert at fooling himself.

I will never be the fool again, he resolved. *Never.*

And just like that, something dark and sinister took over. Glenn felt the heaviness return to his chest, but he ignored it.

Caroline was calling his name. "Glenn. Glenn?"

Glenn? Who's that? He looked at Caroline without emotion.

I'm not Glenn. I'm Radio Rev.

Now she was talking again, trying to dissect their teenage years with psychobabble, rambling on about enlightenment or some other New Age crap. The words flowed freely from her lips, but he ignored the kindness in her voice.

Ignore this seemingly genuine concern. No one's ever cared before! Why should this be any different?

With resolve, he resumed the self-talk he had used successfully through the years: *I am good at this. I was a blocker in football, and I can do it in real life, too. Block out the people who hurt me. Get past the pain as quickly as possible.*

He smoothed out the wrinkles of his suit jacket and tightened his red power tie. *Who did I think I was, coming here today, anyway? People may call that blasted little voice inside your head intuition, but I call it over-rated. Time to go with what I know.*

Rev smiled the smile of every person who had attended the sunrise service at the Radio Rev Revival Weekend and looked at Caroline evenly.

Of course, her beauty is unmistakable, but there's lots of pretty faces in this world. Pretty faces who can be molded. Influenced. Seduced... by me. Who is this Caroline girl, anyway, with her head in the clouds, challenging everything I've been taught? Everything I teach?

"I understand, Caroline. Please excuse my momentary lapse of reason. I guess I got nostalgic, that's all."

With relief evident on her face, Rev continued. The more he spoke, the easier it became to believe his own words. "You know, I may have exaggerated a bit about my feelings, you know. Yes, there was some good on my end from our breakup, too. Yessiree. I've become quite the worker bee, young lady."

Caroline flinched at his words, clearly uncomfortable with the condescending tone.

Rev plowed on, "You may not be aware, but I have single-handedly catapulted a small radio station to the top of the charts. Because of my show, I've been able to bring in unprecedented amounts of money for WFAM and missionaries worldwide!"

He sat up straighter as he witnessed her shifting awkwardly on the couch. Obviously, Caroline couldn't adjust to this swift change in demeanor.

Good, he thought. *She thinks she's so smart, eh? Keep her on her toes.*

"In fact, my success at the station would never have reached such epic proportions if…"

The trilling of his cell phone interrupted them. He glanced at the number and rolled his eyes. "Ugh, it's the WFAM station manager. Excuse me."

Caroline sat, open-mouthed, as Rev stood up to take the call. He listened quietly to the caller and then hung up. She thought he looked worried, but the look flickered across his face so quickly she couldn't be sure.

"Well?" Caroline asked.

"It's nothing, really. Just some business at the station that requires my attention." He paused.

Caroline perked up, sensing a potential story. "Is everything OK?"

He sighed, "It seems that one of the attenders at the revival ran into a bit of a, umm, problem."

Caroline's eyes opened wide. Rev conveniently dodged the full explanation and continued, "And that isn't even the best part. The woman in question is my secretary – from work!"

Before she could ask, he explained, "Oh, yes. I didn't get the chance to tell you – I'm a high school principal, too."

For once, the girl with all the questions had none, for nothing in the last five minutes made any sense. He filled the silence with reassuring words. His voice rose, and several patrons looked over at this man with so much self-confidence.

"Don't worry, dear Caroline," he joked, thinking of his reputation at school. "Even though the kids fear 'Glenn Vambles, The Principal Who Loves Detention,' I'm not that scary. Really, I'm not." The ominous grin Rev wore belied his words, and Caroline looked away from the man she wasn't sure she ever knew at all.

The barista behind the counter stared at this bold person. And in classic Radio Rev style, he spun on his heels and strode out of the coffee shop, leaving a gaping Caroline with the bill.

CHAPTER 29

Broken Pieces

HOPE

June

The bell rang. A folded, white piece of notebook paper lay on the top shelf of my locker. There was no mistaking Karen's special note-folding style. I ripped the paper open as quickly as I could.

> *Ten days down, ten to go! Can't wait to hang out again. Mom is driving me crazy, as usual. How have your parents been treating you? Are you as grounded as I am? Wish our lockers and last period classes were closer.*
>
> *xo Karen*

Had it really been ten days since the revival? Between the talks with our parents and visits to the police station, life as I knew it before was over. The detectives wanted to get statements from Karen and me. First, they met with each of us alone. Then they let us meet together. I didn't understand why they couldn't have talked to us together from the start, but my dad said it had something to do with unblemished testimony.

After all the sneaking around, the last thing I was going to do was lie to the cops, so I told them everything – from Anthony's stories, to Miss Lillian's famous break dancing, to everything that happened that fateful Friday night in the basement.

Following their initial shock, my parents calmed down and talked to me with only a few bouts of screaming (that was from my mom, when she articulated each part of our plan that was "dangerous and stupid" – her words, not mine).

Not surprisingly, the Pandoras banned Karen from everything – that meant no leaving the house, no TV, no phone, no computer. Everything was off-limits until June 15. This time, I had a feeling Mrs. Pandora would stick to the punishment.

And though I wasn't officially grounded, I knew the Saturday night date with Eli was off – at least for now. Luckily, he totally understood why our date would need to be postponed.

I looked at the text again: "Good things come to those who wait." Eli's promising words made me tingle. I could only hope there would be other chances to spend time together: more dances, more time to feel his arms around my waist, more time alone. And kissing? I remembered the sensation of Eli's soft lips on my ear. I couldn't wait to find out how much better a real kiss from him would feel. I just hoped he wouldn't be like some guys at school that I'd heard about: they would rate their girlfriends based on looks, kissing – even things like weight and bra size!

But Eli's not like that. Grateful for the gazillionth time for his maturity, I tucked away my fantasies, knowing I could indulge in them after the Lillian drama subsided.

The sunlight made me squint as I walked out of the dimly lit school. The old yellow busses lined the parking lot, waiting to take us home. I trudged up the steps of bus #51 and sat down, alone. Ever since the incident (as everyone seemed to be calling it), Mrs. Pandora drove

Karen to and from school each day. We didn't even have the brief bus ride home together anymore.

Without anyone decent to talk to, I buried myself in *Finding Your Voice*. I was onto the last chapter, and this one looked like it would be the best: "Know when to express your opinions, and when to remain silent. This is the ultimate dance of life, but if you master it, the world is yours for the taking."

Anthony and his friends filed into the seats across from me. "Hey, Hope," Anthony began, "are you allowed to talk now?" He was referring to the gag order. Since we were a part of the investigation, we were forbidden to talk about the case to anyone – friends included – until Miss Lillian's trial, set for mid-June. No matter what anyone said, I couldn't respond. It could ruin everything if I talked.

Anthony yelled across the aisle to a friend. "Hey, Dude! Since Hope can't talk yet, let's fill in the blanks. Miss Lillian tried to use the church in her basement to kidnap unsuspecting teenagers. But then her evil husband tried to take them and do God-knows-what, but she said, 'I want them all to myself!' and whack – his old lady took care of him!" The other boys laughed.

I fumed. Even though she was far from innocent, they made Miss Lillian sound like a monster. They knew just enough from the news reports to know she was accused of blackmail, endangering minors, and possibly spousal battery, but not enough to feel sympathy for a woman who clearly had problems. I consoled myself with my book. *Know when to remain silent, Hope.*

Anthony continued, making up more and more outrageous accusations. *Why does Karen like him?* I wondered. *Love must be blind because not only isn't Anthony that great-looking, but he's not very kind, either!* Of course, he's not a total jerk like a Krystal or Maddie, but he was not at all considerate of Miss Lillian's feelings.

Everyone's been trying to tell me to stop pitying Miss Lillian, but I can't help it. Karen and I got to see a small slice of her life, and it wasn't pretty. Alcoholic husband, living alone, obsessed with radio church? It didn't sound like fun, and it didn't sound like the hopes and dreams I had for my life. I tried explaining that to my parents a few days after the revival, but they didn't want to listen.

"Hope, this is a person who was brainwashed by a radio evangelist and, in her warped mind, thought it was okay to kidnap you!"

I protested that she hadn't actually kidnapped us. "Oh, right," Mom sneered. "She just threatened to tell your parents if you didn't follow her orders! She played on your fears and knowingly drove you to a revival behind our backs!"

Wow, Mom was angry! It was then I knew I'd have to keep my sympathy for Miss Lillian to myself. Or at least until I could talk to Karen about it.

I imagined Miss Lillian sitting in a jail cell with the other inmates surrounding her. A frostiness that I couldn't explain ran through my veins.

No matter what my parents said, I still couldn't think of her as a criminal. Crazy? Definitely. "Made a bad choice" (as my mom would say to her students)? For sure. But she wasn't out to hurt us, of that I was certain. In some twisted way, she must have thought taking us to that service was good for us. I had no idea how a gospel choir and a pastor's speech were worth all the trouble she went through, but in a weird way I was flattered. *Someone thought enough of me to go to jail for it!*

I attempted to focus on my book. Anything to take my mind off of the incident. Thinking about it made me tired, and there was no use trying to talk about it to my family anymore. It would have to wait until Karen was allowed out in the world again.

The bus squeaked to a stop at the corner of Karen's house. I shoved *Finding Your Voice* into my backpack and stepped off the bus. Peering into Karen's dining room window, I could see her sitting at the table, hunched over what I guessed was her homework.

She must have sensed me, because she looked up and gave a quick wave. Another person entered the room, and Karen's head quickly returned to her work. It was Mrs. Pandora, probably triple-checking on Karen. From surreptitiously passed notes and our twenty-minute lunches, I knew that her mom wasn't letting her out of sight anymore. Not for a second. "It's sooo annoying, Hope! She won't let me go anywhere alone! And I mean anywhere!"

I giggled. "Even the bathroom?"

My laughing faded when Karen nodded.

Turning the corner, I trudged up the hill toward home. A white sedan passed by, and for a moment, my stomach dropped. As I looked closer, I realized the car was new, and the driver was a large man delivering supermarket circulars. He stopped in front of each house, threw the advertisements out of his window, and moved to the next house.

Passing Ms. Parker's house, I gave the woman a little wave. She was outside weeding her flower bed, as usual. She looked around to see who I was waving to. With a confused look, she waved back and then puckered her lips.

Guess she can't understand that someone is just waving a friendly hello! But I had found myself doing that a lot lately – waving to ladies who seemed sad and lonely.

I unlocked the front door and walked inside the empty house, glad for a few minutes alone before anyone else returned from work or school. I went upstairs to my room and opened the closet door. It took a few minutes to fish the box out from its hiding place, but when I got it, I sat with it on my lap. Gold letters of the famous jewelry store stood out against the black wooden box. I opened it, and even though I had looked at it hundreds of times before, what I saw inside still took my breath away. It looked even better now than it did that night in the basement when Karen and I got our first glimpse of Paul's gift. The two beautiful, glittering earrings sparkled against the creamy velvet interior, and a piece of folded paper filled the back of the box. But I didn't need to unfold the note to know what it said.

Dear Hope,

I can't tell you how sorry I am about all of this. I just wanted to save you and Karen. I thought you needed it even more than Karen, but now I know I'm the one who needs the saving. Please accept this as an apology from me for putting you through all of this. The enclosed box is what Paul had in his back pocket that night. He was trying to win me back and thought the gift would help. For years, I wanted a beautiful pair of solitaire earrings, but Paul thought jewelry gifts were stupid. Guess he was trying to change his ways!

Good news, though: he really is trying to change… I heard he went to his first AA meeting last week. Anyway, please know that you and Karen did nothing wrong. You were just curious – that's all. And I hope at some point you can find it in your heart to forgive me.

Take care and God bless,

Lillian Amadon

I don't know how she got it delivered to me from jail – but there it was, sitting on the top shelf of my locker last Monday morning, the same place where Karen would leave me notes. This was the one thing I hadn't shared with anyone, not even Karen. My parents would be furious if they knew she sent it. They probably would think she was still stalking me, but something told me this was the first and last time she would be in touch. Somehow, I knew this was her sorry and goodbye, all rolled into one.

Keys jiggled in the front door. *Mom.* I scrambled to put the box back into its hiding place. I concealed the box just as she entered the foyer and yelled hello. But my mind was on Lillian and the earrings.

Mom stood in the doorway. "Doing homework?"

I paused and then nodded yes. My mother didn't like secrecy, and I knew at some point I would probably end up telling Mom about the earrings.

Just not today.

RADIO REV

June 10

Everything in the past two weeks had been a blur. However, several moments would be etched in his mind forever, such as hopping into his car to race back to the WFAM revival – not because he was getting there early for the next sermon, but because Radio Rev had a date with the police. They were curious to find out if there were any connections between Lillian Amadon and the principal-by-day/evangelist-by-night.

Other unanswered questions plagued the investigators following Lillian's confession. For example, did Glenn Vambles, a.k.a. Radio Rev, have any idea why his secretary blackmailed two Roosevelt students? That one he could answer honestly with a resounding *No.*

When he arrived at the huge white tent, two undercover detectives escorted him into a dark, unmarked police car. It was then that Rev realized the police were more than a little suspicious about his involvement with this whole mess. Suzanne's look of disappointment was unmistakable as he drove away from WFAM's makeshift headquarters. Due to the unfortunate turn of events, the rest of the weekend had to be cancelled, but he could have cared less at the moment.

Luckily for him, the police found no link between Lillian Amadon and Glenn Vambles other than their working relationship. Once he felt certain the police found him to be a credible witness, he began to rest easy, knowing that the only person in danger of jail time was Lillian.

The Monday following the revival fiasco, the station president had called to tell the reverend how sorry he was, but didn't he understand that any scandal from the investigation might spell disaster for WFAM? Wouldn't he like to take a little vacation? In fact, the president suggested, he could make Radio Rev a sweet offer to return to his hometown and take over the leading spot on their fledgling radio enterprise there.

He couldn't believe his ears. *I, Radio Rev, was the one who put WFAM on the map! Who are they to force me to leave?* But he considered the president's position and knew his boss had a point.

Rev spent that evening exploring his options. He researched the income levels of the top-rated evangelists, and the information astounded him. *If I'm even half as successful as these idiots, I'll be making more than I was at Roosevelt and WFAM combined!*

Now Rev was sitting at his desk, tidying files and putting personal effects into a black plastic crate. Ever since the news broke, his days at school were filled with calls and impromptu visits from parents, students, and the media. Overnight, he had transitioned from a religious radio-station hero to a mainstream media darling. Here was a man who, somehow, concealed his identity as a public school principal while moonlighting as a larger-than-life radio evangelist, and never had the two paths crossed. Until now.

How did he keep those lives separate? That was the question the curious, microphone-pushing reporters asked most frequently. He did his best to explain that it was his insistence on anonymity as Radio Rev that afforded him the ability to do both and not blur his secular position with his religious one.

He purposely failed to mention the way he could turn off his southern accent at school and turn it back on for broadcasts. Likewise, he "forgot" to tell them that there was enough distance between the station's offices in Philadelphia and the New Jersey suburb in which he worked to allow the identity of the Rev to remain shrouded in mystery. And of course, utilizing The Voice to draw in listener support simply "slipped his mind" during the police interrogation.

Even without all of the information, the reporters loved the principal-gone-underground angle, and parents and students were obsessed with the news. Though it was difficult to make his way through the school day with any sense of normalcy, Radio Rev didn't mind. He had more important things to think about, anyway.

Within forty-eight hours, his life had taken several major turns. First, with the revival's cancellation and less-than-stellar donations at the sunrise service, it must have been the final straw for Suzanne, for she quickly tendered her resignation. The last he heard, she was in the final interview process at WKOL, the popular oldies station.

Next, he made a call to his father. Without going into detail, he mentioned the idea of heading back home to help out their local radio station. Knowing that his hometown was a segment of the world that was insulated from anything that would be considered mainstream, he knew there was no danger of them learning about this little blemish on his pastoral record. He figured his dad, of all people, didn't need to know too much, either. He was too proud of his son.

Why cause him any worry or concern? Let him think I'm homesick, and then I can simply pick up where I left off.

He visualized all the doting fans he would have just from his home church. He could almost picture the dollar signs and donation records he would break. And beautiful women, just waiting for the meaningful words of an important man of the cloth... *Maybe I can get a little slice of the action this time? Get the girl, make some real money, and live the good life, like some of those big names on television. Who says radio personalities can't be rich? Look at those shock jocks who make their money from cursing! I can do the same thing – with prayer.*

He had reached the last two files in the cabinet. He paused when he held the oldest one with a "C" on the front, and then quickly, before he could change his mind, jammed the file into the shredder. Years of research turned into newspaper pasta as the pages passed through the shredder's slicing blades. The last file didn't have a single mark on it, but he knew why. This was his "power of suggestion" file – the one some critics might call brainwashing. But from this day forward, he vowed to think of it merely as the secret to success. *No one shares secret recipes, right? Neither do I.* Into the shredder it went, for Radio Rev already knew how to get people to listen. He had mastered the technique.

The next day, to the silent cheers of the students and to the chagrin of parents who liked good, old-fashioned discipline, Principal Vambles made his resignation official, effective immediately. He kept his announcement simple, focusing on the importance of the school returning to a state of normalcy and halting the carnival-like atmosphere that was threatening to become a permanent presence in the building.

In his *People* magazine interview (they dubbed him "Most Mysterious Man of the Year"), he allowed them access to his double life, as they loved to call it. *Ahh, the media.* How they loved to take his relatively boring life and turn it into an espionage-sounding lifestyle. Principal by day! Preacher by night! Extra, extra! Read all about it!

As he read the article, he laughed out loud several times. Somehow, he wished his real life were as exciting as they made his magazine life out to be. He noticed that with a talented reporter, something as simple as walking the halls at Roosevelt High could appear deliciously exciting and enviable.

Instead of worrying too much about fact and fiction, he allowed the reporters to do their job. His only mandate was that they could never – ever! – mention Lillian Amadon's name in conjunction with his. For that transgression, he threatened every camera-toting paparazzi member a swift lawsuit and the wrath of a religious machine that could rival Judgment Day. He must have convinced them he was serious, because no article had ever mentioned the secretary's name, and for the reverend, that made it even easier to pretend the whole incident never happened.

Amidst the media melee, the front office ladies were also dealing with the fallout of being one secretary short. All of Lillian's work had gone to the second-in-command, a competent but very nervous Sarah Lee. Sarah Lee seemed shocked by the new responsibilities foisted on her, and she was yet another person who constantly interrupted the principal's thoughts and work to ask questions.

He knew that life, in an unexpected way, had been good to him lately, because instead of the secretaries showing resentment over the extra work, they seemed delighted. It must have had something to do with his insistence that, in the magazine shoot, he made certain every secretary was featured in the picture. *Ah, a little manipulation never hurts, does it?*

Some of the extra phone calls the school was receiving came from adoring relatives and friends who were impressed at the secretaries' newfound fame. They were flattered enough that they didn't give their boss or the other reporters waiting in the front office too many dirty looks for inconveniencing their normally-busy days. As they gushed to the reporters about the hassles of their daily grind, Rev congratulated himself again. *You certainly know how to put people at ease, from radio listeners, to secretaries. Get them to do your bidding. Why was I so shy about my success before? Must've been those memories of what's-her-name bringing me down.*

He glanced up at the office calendar, courtesy of the local pizza parlor. That month displayed a picture of an older Italian woman in a kitchen, while birds flew by the window of a European-looking house. He had circled one date – June 15. Lillian's court date.

A few days before, he had visited Lillian in jail. The detectives were still sifting through the increasingly-complicated case, taking statements from everyone and sorting it all out. When she walked up to the Plexiglas divider and picked up the phone to hear his voice, her face shined with optimism. "Rev! I mean, Principal Vambles! How are you? I can't believe that you were the voice I had been listening to, day after day. And to think you were right next door, the whole time!" For a minute, Lillian looked as if she forgot she were in jail. Her smile brightened, and he took this as his cue to begin.

After insisting she call him Reverend instead of Principal Vambles, he tried to explain to Lillian how nothing he did in any way related to her religious life – or impending court date. He made his voice sound equally sad and encouraging. Understanding yet firm.

With a sympathetic smile, he stated his rehearsed lines: "Lillian, I feel your pain. Lord knows I do! But in uncertain times, the Devil may try to confuse that lovely mind of yours and implicate me, of all people, in your unfortunate situation. I just want to say…"

Lillian interrupted her former boss. "Listen, we're adults. You made your choices, and I made mine. I don't hold anything against you."

His look of doubt caused her to repeat, "Really, I don't hold you responsible!" She paused. "But, I hope you'll understand if I don't want to follow your program anymore."

That's it? That's her idea of a punishment?

He nodded, trying to look truly disappointed. *Does she really think her paltry twenty-dollar donations mean a lick to me?*

She continued, "To be completely frank, I think I was a better person before your show came into my life. I don't mean to be disrespectful,

Mr. Vambles – I mean Reverend – but you deliver a heavy message, and I guess I took it to heart."

He didn't like hearing her say that she was a better person before, but, *hey, this was a freak, right?* His stomach relaxed as he realized she had no intentions of involving him in her crazy life.

Guess I can be magnanimous then. Turn on that charm, Rev... "Lillian, I hope you know, I never meant to –"

She cut him off again. "I know, I know. You didn't mean for me to save souls in the way I did! Believe me, I get it now. But for some reason, oh, I don't know...loneliness after Paul left, depression, who knows? For some reason I just went off the deep end. And it's cost me my life, for the most part. Who knows how guilty a jury may find me? And how punitive a judge might be?"

The reverend shivered, thinking about Lillian and her possible jail time. He was glad he would be able to leave this unstable woman soon.

Unbelievably, Lillian smiled. "But it's alright, Glenn – can I call you that?" He bristled, but Lillian didn't notice. "I'm coming to terms with everything, and I mean it when I say I don't blame you. But you're going to have to count on donations from another source at WFAM from now on."

In the awkward silence that followed her generous proclamations, he considered telling her that he was quitting the station, but then thought better of it. And he really wanted to remind her – for the second time – that his name was Rev. Not Glenn. Not Principal Vambles. But logic and reason won out: *I've gotta watch my words. Anything that upsets this nitwit's routine may send her into another tailspin!* He had overheard the detectives talking, and he was sure he heard the words "bipolar disorder".

Radio Rev wasn't stupid. He wasn't going to do anything to toy with a fragile psyche. *But I'm sure a compliment wouldn't hurt to ensure she isn't looking to blame me for anything...*

"Lillian, I think you're a wonderful person with a big heart. I hope and pray that a judge and jury will be compassionate."

No one could have misread the smile on Lillian's face, and he thought triumphantly, *This is almost too easy! Why did I fight my natural talents before? I was born to convince people to follow me.*

He went in for the kill: "So, if there's anything I can do…"

She pounced on the offer, as if she had been waiting all day for him to mention it. "Well, there is just one favor…" she began.

As he listened, he regretted his proposal to help this whackadoodle. Not only did she want him to go into her house and take what he was positive the police would consider evidence, but she wanted him to deliver it to a student!

He considered her request for hours, and in the end, he decided that this would be the insurance plan he was looking for. If he did her this favor, he was confident that she would leave him alone, never again to contact him. And that would be one more unsavory part of his life he could file away and ignore.

No time for the people of this town anymore. I've got a long-lost home-town filled with congregants who miss me and my irresistible religious message!

Since Lillian's husband had already made it clear that he was supporting Lillian through the trial, the Rev wasn't overly worried about his former secretary's request. Even though she was asking him to tamper with possible evidence, he was sure the husband's testimony would carry more weight than the two-carat diamonds she asked him to fetch.

So, Rev found the hide-a-key behind the shed just as she directed and let himself into the Amadon bungalow. After finding the earrings, he decided the best way to handle it was to continue to be as anonymous as possible. The next day, he slid the box gently into the top shelf of Hope's locker, as requested by Lillian, along with the note Lillian had given to him that day from the jail.

He held his breath as he watched the monitors in the freshman hallway that day. In the grainy security cameras, he saw Hope fumble with her lock amidst the sea of students going to their lockers. Then he saw her reach in, take out the box, and look around suspiciously. He exhaled as he watched her open the note, scan it, and then carefully place the box and letter in the bottom of her backpack. As if she sensed she were being watched, she looked around one more time before heading out of the building. *Smart girl,* he thought. *Knows which secrets are worth keeping.*

Epilogue

HOPE

June 10

Life had finally returned to normal. Karen was almost ungrounded, Ms. Tievel was boring as ever, and my parents were back to falling asleep on the sofa on Friday nights. Even all the excitement surrounding Mr. Vambles, a.k.a. Radio Rev, had faded. Once again, the principal blended in with the scenery, except for the times when the occasional reporter would visit the school for a follow-up story. Word was that there might be an investigation into Radio Rev's knowledge (or lack thereof) concerning his secretary's plan. Through it all, he denied any complicity in the case. In fact, the rumors in the halls hinted at an announcement that he would be leaving town, pronto.

The last we heard about Miss Lillian was that she was awaiting a summer trial, and her lawyers were going to try to prove that her newly-diagnosed mental illnesses drove her to blackmail us that fateful day. When I heard that, part of my mind said, "Excuses, excuses!" but another part of me, the kinder part, I guess, believed that only a crazy person would have done those things. Since it was all just too confusing, I decided to push it to the back of my mind and deal with more important things, like my huge week of exams and Cyrinda's insane birthday party that was quickly becoming the talk of the school.

At first, I thought the crowd of students at the water fountain was a group of people waiting for a drink. But when I caught a glimpse of Neha Asan, I slowed my walking. Everyone knew Neha and her family were strict Muslims, and the robes she wore to school drew attention to that fact. Personally, I liked Neha and her beautiful robes that sometimes had small diamond-looking jewels stitched to them. I wouldn't have wanted to wear them in the eighty-degree weather and even hotter classrooms, but her garb seemed interestingly exotic to me. Unfortunately, not everyone respected Neha's uniqueness. On any given day, I could hear kids snickering as she walked by, or worse, when someone would purposely stand on her robe, bringing her to an abrupt halt as she moved through the hall.

Most times, I would ignore it. I know, I know, all of our teachers told us not to be bystanders in these instances, but some days, I was just so glad it wasn't me they were ridiculing. Those kids were going to bully whoever they could, and though I wasn't proud of my silence, I knew lots of other kids did the same thing.

Today was different, though. It wasn't the normal group of boys making comments or sticking their feet out. No, it was Cyrinda Lovegaarten. Yes, that was her real name! And before you laugh, let me tell you more – she was a top student at school, well-liked by just about everyone, and her parents made huge donations to the community ever since they moved in last year.

Apparently, Mr. Lovegaarten was some big Hollywood director who had tired of LA. So he moved East, wanting to be close enough to New York to continue his work while escaping the killer traffic and fast-paced city life. When Mrs. Lovegaarten discovered a sprawling mansion in the New Jersey suburbs that fit both of their tastes perfectly, Cyrinda became Maddie Braun's rival in the "richest student" category.

Yes, everyone loved the Lovegaartens – teachers, students, little kids, old ladies, even dogs! It was like Cyrinda and her family were almost too good to be true. I mean, how many girls living in mansions are down-to-earth and friendly? Karen and I got to know Cyrinda from working on the school newspaper together, and now we had plans to attend her much-talked-about birthday party.

But now Cyrinda was standing next to Neha, obviously engaged in a serious discussion. A group of students gathered around to listen. From what I could see, most of the kids who had surrounded them were shy, quiet students. No Krystal or Maddie in sight. But then I heard Cyrinda's voice.

"Neha, what I'm trying to say is that your god isn't real. Isn't that right, girls?" She didn't wait for the friends to respond. "Your robes are pretty cool, but why don't you come to church with me this week? We can get you hooked up with the real thing!" She smiled, waiting expectantly for Neha's reply.

Before I knew it, I found myself pushing two girls out of the way and entering the human circle of students. I walked up to Cyrinda and started screaming at her. Cyrinda's eyes widened to saucer-like proportions as I laid into her. I don't even know exactly what I said: something about *stop trying to make everyone the same... stop trying to say who's right and who's wrong...* all I remembered was ending with a screeching, "Stop judging her! Who do you think you are?" And with that, I stormed off.

I ran into the girls' bathroom and locked myself in a stall. The metal door felt cold through my thin T-shirt, and the tears that streamed down my face burned my cheeks. *Why did I do that? Cyrinda's friends with me, and she wasn't being intentionally mean.* I could tell from the look on her face that she actually believed her words and probably didn't find them offensive.

In the distance, I could hear teachers yelling at kids to get to class, Ms. Tievel's nasally voice asking Cyrinda what happened. I didn't even listen to her reply – I didn't care what Cyrinda had to say at the moment. A small knock startled me into a standing position. Someone was knocking on my stall! I peeked through the sliver between the door and wall. Grey hair and silk filled the crack. *Ms. Tievel.*

It's probably like the police – the less you fight, the easier they make things for you. I opened the door, wiping the tears with the back of my hand. Surprisingly, Ms. Tievel was smiling.

"Hope, I must say I'm a little surprised at your outburst. That's not really like you, is it?"

I shrugged my shoulders. I figured the less ammunition I gave her, the less she could use against me.

"Well, I think what you said was spot-on. You stood up for that student's religious freedom, and I'm proud of you! I guess the 'incident' with Lillian Amadon really made an impression on you, and I mean that in a good way. You now know what it feels like to be the object of persecution, don't you?"

Huh? The incident? Persecution? What does Miss Lillian have to do with anything? Rather than argue with Ms. Tievel, something no one with any common sense wants to do anyway, I mustered a fake smile and thanked her, hoping she would let me wash my face before returning to class.

After another congratulations and disturbing pat on the back, she left me alone one more time. I looked in the mirror. *Will Cyrinda hate me for that?* I waited for the feeling of dread to wash over me because someone might dislike me, but I felt nothing. My whole body felt clear, like something dark and evil was released in the hallway. I almost expected to see a black cloud float away as I opened the door, but seeing nothing, I dragged myself down the corridor toward Spanish class.

Bienvenido! read the pre-fab poster on the door of Senora Paola's room. *Welcome.*

Yes, I thought, *maybe welcoming others is something we all can do.*

EPILOGUE

Our teacher was rapidly reviewing verb conjugations for an upcoming test. I sat down and tried to concentrate, but it was impossible. *I already know soy, eres, es, somos, son. She's probably just being nice to the Nate Geromes of the world who need some extra practice.*

I allowed my mind to roam. I began thinking about my future. Not the future the guidance counselors always ask us to consider, like filling out college applications and getting scholarships. No, I was thinking about my new future, the one that excited me since reading *Finding Your Voice*. Confronting Cyrinda confirmed what I already knew: I had changed, and *that* could change everything.

Like, my parents never keep their opinions to themselves, and I've always just gone with the flow, even when I don't agree with them. It just seemed easier, especially when I'd listen to the screaming matches between Patrick and my mom. But I'm ready to try something new. As in, the next time I don't like their views, I'm going to tell them. Even if it starts a mini-World War III! Patrick might even thank me for taking the heat off him.

I've also noticed that now, instead of obsessing over what everyone thinks about me, I'm beginning to consider my own opinions. I know, novel concept, right? Actually thinking about how I feel about something! I have a feeling that people at school are going to start respecting me more for having my own opinions. At the very least, I know I'll respect myself more.

Yeah, Cyrinda will probably be pissed with me for a week or two, but even that will fade over time. Disagreeing with her doesn't mean I don't like her. And what about those crazy worries I had about people hating me for being imperfect? It's never happened in reality, and it probably never will. *Why didn't I ever notice that before?* I smiled, resolving to enjoy life rather than approach it with anxiety and apprehension. *I am going to go to Cyrinda's party with my head held high.*

Even boys aren't intimidating me as much as they once did. Sure, I can be dorky, but Eli's going to have to get used to that if he wants to spend time with me. Besides, he can be corny, too. I mean, he puts all these cute emoticons of smiley faces and animals when he texts me. What "cool" guy does that? But I don't mind. Not at all!

And why am I so worried about what Eli might try with me? I can make my own decisions, regardless of what parents or friends tell me. Ultimately, I am going to be the person that I want to be, and no empty promise of popularity or acceptance will sidetrack me from that. *Maybe these next four years will be some of the best of my life after all!*

I felt a tap on my shoulder followed by a stab from the corner of a folded-up note being jabbed into my back. I grabbed the paper, being careful to hide most of it under my worksheet. It was from Karen.

What happened? I thought we were going to Cyrinda's party together! Are we mad at her for some reason? I giggled, enjoying the fact that Karen was so loyal to me that she would be angry with Cyrinda if I thought we had good reason. *Are 'we' mad at her?*

I scribbled a hasty, *No, I'll explain later,* and returned the note, holding my breath and hoping that Senora Paola wouldn't notice. With the note safely passed, I tried to figure out what, exactly, I needed to explain to Karen.

But instead of thinking of an explanation, I made a decision. After school, I would figure out a way to mail those earrings back to Miss Lillian. Getting rid of the beautiful jewelry would be the best decision I'd made lately. Then, I could tell Mom about it, and she'd be relieved that I didn't have the jewelry in my possession anymore. After all of that, I'd think of a way to deal with Cryinda. After *I* figured out why I freaked out in the first place.

Ms. Tievel, proud of me? I glanced at my Language Arts Notebook with the hastily-scrawled quote Ms. Tievel forced us to copy last week:

"When the student is ready, the teacher will appear."

I chewed on the eraser end of my pencil and, for some inexplicable reason, felt the need to say a silent thank you to Miss Lillian. For the second time that day, the air cleared, and I turned my attention back to my schoolwork. I even sketched a heart on my composition book with the name "Eli" written in the middle. *Time to let the Lillian chapter in my life close and get back to my new, improved life!*

LILLIAN
June 12

The thump of the mailbox startled Lillian. *That shouldn't surprise me. The mailman always delivers at two.* Without a job to return to, Lillian had quickly become attuned to the daily sounds and schedule of life at home all day. Part of her relished the imposed solitude. People couldn't attack her with questions the way they would if she were back at Roosevelt. Another part of her missed human contact, though. Even the brief phone calls with Paul from the Re-Vitalize Rehab did little to keep her company through the lonely hours of each day.

Lillian picked herself up from the couch and tore her eyes away from the daytime talk show. Three ladies were getting ready to have a make-over, and all they could do was giggle and babble about how nervous they were. *Ladies, you don't even know what nervous is until you're faced with possible jail time.* She said another silent thank you to Paul and the detectives who spoke so kindly on her behalf, allowing her to be released from jail "on her own recognizance" before her June 15 trial date.

She walked to the door and looked at the pile of mail that Ned Hardings slid through her old-fashioned mail slot. A small box wrapped in a brown paper bag wedged the slot open. Lillian carefully pried the box through the slot and held the lightweight package in her hand. With trembling hands, she tore off the paper. Gold letters peeked through, and her heart sank. Tears formed behind her eyes.

"She didn't want it," Lillian whispered.

For the rest of the day, Lillian wandered from room to room in a trance, reliving the events of the past year in her mind. When she finally thought about the package, she decided to finish unwrapping it. She hadn't noticed it at first, but a small note was tucked into the box along with the earrings. Not sure if she wanted to read it, she held the box in her hands as if it may explode.

"Oh, what the heck," she sighed when she couldn't stand the suspense any longer. The heart-shaped paper was strawberry-scented. Hope's loopy cursive sprawled across the page in purple pen:

Miss Lillian,

I wanted to thank you for the earrings. They are beautiful… I can't believe you wanted me to have them! But as much as I love them, I can't keep your generous present. They were a gift to you from Mr. Amadon, and I'm sure he'd want to see you wearing them. Please accept my re-gift as a thank you. Good luck with your trial. We'll be rooting for you!

Hope

Thank you? For what?
Lillian sat in that chair for hours, as the sun set that afternoon and the shadows of evening crossed over the wooden floorboards, until finally she sat in darkness with the outside streetlamp illuminating the room. Though she may never know the reason, she sensed that the forgiveness from a fourteen-year-old girl might give her strength she needed for the days ahead.

Strength, she thought – *and Hope.*

CAROLINE

Caroline had walked home slowly that evening from the coffee shop, deciding to skip her evening yoga class. After a quick text to let Paige know she'd have to do her sun salutations alone this week, Caroline walked past the doorman. He called after her, "No elevator today, Miss Richards?"

She dazzled him with her brilliant smile. "Not today, Gerald. I'll take the steps."

With each step she took, Caroline summarized the facts from the Glenn Vambles puzzle. She had always found this fact-finding method helpful in uncovering the truth with complicated news stories. Maybe it would help her now.

Step. *Left Georgia to teach Social Studies in New Jersey.* Step. *Became a principal and eventually a radio pastor – not a huge surprise for a minister's kid.* Step. *Left some sort of revival to come see me. Made it sound like he was interested in picking up where we left off with our high school romance.* Step. *Did an about-face when I told him I wasn't interested and then started bragging about being some hot-shot pastor and a "not-so-scary" principal.*

She reached the landing and stopped. Something in Glenn's voice had unsettled Caroline. There was a musical, rhythmic quality to it that she didn't recall from high school. She thought more about his words, and her journalistic instincts screamed, "Bullshit!" *But what was B.S. and what was real in Glenn's story?*

Knowing her answers were more likely to come to her as she relaxed her mind and focused on other issues, Caroline turned her attention to the letter from her book editor. She wanted Caroline to update the copy of her best-selling book. "Let's reprint this as the 'ten-year edition.' Update it with current examples and new advice. Give the old readers some relevant updates and bring in a young, hip audience."

As her debut book, Caroline held a special place in her heart for this piece. Every word of the self-help book came from personal experience. In fact, a lot of her life lessons resulted from the gut-wrenching break-up with Glenn and the shabby treatment from the students and teachers of Mountwell High School. Though criticized by some reviewers as clichéd advice, Caroline felt confident that this book was her own crowning achievement. It allowed her to create a blueprint for resilience and personal success, and she hoped she could be a role model for others, especially teenage girls.

Updating the book to inspire a new audience is a brilliant idea.

Caroline walked over to the bookshelf and pulled out the first copy of the original, hardcover edition. Book in hand, she padded across the room and sank into her bed, pulling the down comforter around her body. She switched on the light of her bedside table and stared at the cover, the one she had the artist fix at least three times.

The first time, the expression on her face looked ridiculous. "Bert!" she had laughed, "I look like I'm going to kill the reader, not give her advice!" The next time, he got the picture of her right, but the background colors were all wrong. The third time was Caroline's fault. Her agent wanted the book titled *Girl Power!* and Caroline went along with the argument that the title was sure to lead to huge sales. But huge sales weren't all that Caroline was about, so the third time she returned to the cover artist, she proclaimed, "Change that title, Bert! But don't tell my agent – she'll get to see it soon enough."

She tried to predict how her agent would react to the title change. *I'm sure she'll have a few choice words for me, but I love it!* She looked at the title again, as if seeing it for the first time: *Finding Your Voice, by Caroline Richards.*

She yawned. *It's been a long day. I'll begin the revisions tomorrow.* She flipped off the light and pulled the comforter up to her chin.

EPILOGUE

Caroline slept fitfully that night, but the last thing she remembered before drifting off was the sound of her radio, playing softly in the background. She must have bumped the dial, for the station had changed, and all she could hear was an eerie, unsettling male voice that sounded vaguely familiar.

About the Author

Julie C. Lyons is a novelist, teacher, and ghostwriter who lives in New Jersey with her husband and two children. *Chasing Hope* is her debut novel, the first in the soon-to-be released Hidden Hills series.

Julie's love of writing began in sixth grade when she wrote her first book: *There's Always a First Time* was the story of a girl who fell victim to peer pressure and became addicted to drugs. Her first book reviewer (a.k.a. – the girl sitting behind her in class) gave a five-star review that the story was "cool". In that moment, Julie realized that she could be a writer!

When she isn't writing, teaching, or chauffeuring her children to sporting events, Julie can be found playing the piano, skiing, and reading true crime, thrillers, and self-help books.

Julie invites you to connect with her and see chapter samples from her upcoming books at **www.booksforteensbyJulie.com**

Did you enjoy reading Chasing Hope?

If you enjoyed reading this book, please consider leaving a review on Amazon.com so others may easily find this book. If there was something that you would like to see changed or improved, please send us a note at: publisher@booksforteensbyJulie.com

Thank you!